STARFALL

PACIFIC FORCE
BOOK 2

BLAZE WARD

KNOTTED ROAD PRESS

Starfall
Pacific Force, Book 2
Blaze Ward
Copyright © 2023 Blaze Ward
All rights reserved
Published by Knotted Road Press
www.KnottedRoadPress.com

ISBN: 978-1-64470-337-3

Cover art:
Photo 132766342 / Black Suv © Maryna Konoplytska | Dreamstime.com

Cover and interior design copyright © 2023 Knotted Road Press

Reviews
It's true. Reviews help. Even a short one, such as, "Loved it!" So please consider reviewing this book (and all of the ones you've read) on your favorite retailer site.

Never miss a release!
If you'd like to be notified of new releases, sign up for my newsletter.

http://www.blazeward.com/newsletter/

Buy More!
Did you know that you can buy directly from the Knotted Road Press website?

https://www.knottedroadpress.com/shop/

This book is licensed for your personal enjoyment only. All rights reserved. This is a work of fiction. All characters and events portrayed in this book are fictional, and any resemblance to real people or incidents is purely coincidental. This book, or parts thereof, may not be reproduced in any form without permission.

ALSO BY BLAZE WARD

The Science Officer Series

Start with: The Science Officer

The Jessica Keller Chronicles

Start with: Auberon

CS-405 (Command Centurion Kosnett, part of Jessica)

Start with: Queen Anne's Revenge

First Centurion Kosnett (sequel to Jessica)

Start with: Encounter at Vilahana

Additional Alexandria Station Stories

Alexandria Station Collection

Handsome Rob (Alexandria Station Universe)

Start with: Can't Shoot Straight Gang

======================

Corsac Fox

Start with: Flight of the Corsac Fox

Operation Marrakesh

Start with: Trial by Leviathan

Captain Daring

Start with: Revoked

The Hunter Bureau

Start with: Mirrors

Fairchild

Start with: Fairchild

Last Stand

Start with: Lost Dreams

The Lazarus Alliance

Start with: Escape

Shadow of the Dominion

Start with: Longshot Hypothesis

Star Dragon

Start with: Birth of the Star Dragon

Kincaide's War

Start with: The Eden Package

Star Tribes

Start with: Winterstar

ACTION-ADVENTURE

Pacific Force

Start with: Pacific Force

The Red Branch

Start with: Night Strike

Swordmistress Zhen

Start with: Traveler From The West

FANTASTICAL

The Gunderson Case Files, Volume 1

Augustus Derlyth, Occult Detective

Start with: Ill Tidings

NATHANIEL REALLY, really hated quoting Dickens, but looking around the room, he supposed that bastard had nailed this scene square on, no matter how long that man had been dead.

Best of times. Worst of times.

Nathaniel had spent fifteen years as a criminal of one stripe or another. Since he was eighteen, really. He'd seen the highs and the lows over that stretch. At least he wasn't in prison.

Still, Nathaniel wondered if he was the only sane person in this enormous room, which really was saying something. It felt mostly like auditorium made from a vast storage space that had been emptied. Or not filled yet. Concrete walls prefabbed somewhere, then stood up like cards. Way high ceiling. About thirty bodies around him, many of them unshowered today with that particular funk you got when folks didn't eat healthy or exercise enough.

The man known to everyone as *Lord Wraith* was talking over at that end of the room. Bombasting, if Nathaniel could invent a new word to cover it, because English didn't have anything even remotely close.

Probably intended to be a pep talk for his troops, but it came across a little too deranged for Nathaniel, who again wondered how he'd ended up here.

On the one hand, quoting Dickens, it probably was the best of times, though that was a low bar as far as Nathaniel was concerned. He wasn't in an English prison. Hadn't gotten his head shaved or throw in solitary by British Intelligence services. Again.

Nor traded home to the Americans. Gods knows what the CIA, DIA, NSA, FBI, DoD, Treasury, or anybody else would have offered for his butt to be sent back to the States for them to get their hands on him. Those folks had absolutely no sense of humor.

On the other hand, it might also be the worst of times. Until Pacific Force had finally stopped him the first time two years ago, he'd been huge in the dark web where folks had traded information, favors, and merchandise beyond the ken of those fools willing to work for lame-ass government salaries. Then prison. Then out and captured again, escaping two months ago.

Back then, he'd even known when to get out and launder all his ill-gotten gains into legitimate cash. Still, two years in a British prison had meant that he had mostly missed the early days of the cryptocurrency era, where a hundred thousand dollars in investments might have turned him into a paper billionaire.

Nathaniel assumed it was all a Dutch Tulip scam waiting to unravel at some point. Real money was backed by governments. Insured, even, if something happened and you were robbed. Or the bank was.

All the various cryptos were just numbers on a screen. One of these days, electronic demons like him would start hacking into poorly secured online wallets in badly coded coin exchanges, emptying the contents, and turning them into gold at some Saudi ATM where they honest-to-freaking-Allah dispensed bar stock, leaving you with absolutely no way to track that cash whatsoever.

For now, Nathaniel stood towards the back of the room as Lord Wraith, real name Sergi Prova—at least Nathaniel thought so—yammered about a new future for mankind to the folks listening. Mostly new recruits, plus many of the man's officers.

Other officers. Nathaniel had fit in there somewhere.

Today's *chat* was about how technology itself had gone all wrong and threatened to bring down the wrath of… somebody. That part was kind of vague in that charismatic charlatan bullshit stream that reminded Nathaniel far too much of a current American President with a dead ferret on his head.

Had the world gone completely, fucking nuts while he'd been in prison?

Trick question. It had started way earlier than that. All the different flavors of crazy were finally running into each other because the internet let any fool with an opinion find like-minded crazies to share. The resulting gumbo was toxic, because too many other people were making bank grifting all these stupid sons of bitches out of their retirement money.

Still, it had some benefits.

On Nathaniel's immediate right, a stunning brunette in skin-right, black-leather-everything listened raptly as Sergi carried on. She was just enough in front of him that Nathaniel could watch her from the corner of his eye without turning his head and catching Lord Wraith's attention.

Tall. Almost as tall as Nathaniel's six-foot-one, though her shiny combat boots might have extra heel in them. Body like a gymnast with strong thighs, waspish waist that might be a corset from the way her top moved, nice chest, broad shoulders. Long black hair down now but worn up when she needed to work.

Lady Nix, though he hadn't figured out her real name yet. Nobody here had real names. No, everyone here seemed to think of themselves in terms of comic book villains.

Weren't none of them heroes, that was for sure.

Lady Nix was an assassin. And a dangerous maniac who wore a pair of burst-capable Beretta 93R pistols on her hips in fast-draw holsters like some crazed American Cowboy, though her accent was one hundred percent London toff. What fool needed that kind of firepower in each hand? Assassins Nathaniel had known—the good ones—usually needed a single-shot .22 pistol and exceptional patience.

Glancing around, the others listening to the madman up front were just as bad. Some woman called *Grim Motoko*. Another female with a knife fetish who went by *Dead Eve*. Another probable female named *Neon Scoundrel* dressed as something of a court jester. Nathaniel had no interest in *confirming* their plumbing one way or another.

Were all Lord Wraith's hired killers women? Maybe. Nathaniel didn't want to know what that said. Not today.

And even Nathaniel had been forced to get into the act as part of his employment contract, so they called him *Moriarty*.

Nathaniel wondered if anybody here had enough literary background to actually know the character from the books, rather than any of the video remakes over the last however long.

Best of times, sure. Not in prison. Always a win, when

angry bureaucrats had a chance to get even for being embarrassed so many times.

Worst of times, looking around. Nathaniel was a high-ranking mid-lister in this organization. This thing Lord Wraith called his *Dark Citizen Movement.*

But it was painfully clear that he had become the one thing Nathaniel Hoestler swore he would never settle for. Ever.

A minion.

Fuck that noise.

Lord Wraith took a renewing breath as the current diatribe wound to a pause.

Tall man. Rangy thing. Former punk musician from the late seventies who was in his mid-fifties now. At least if he really was Sergi. Blond beard that was mostly dyed these days. Shaved head with the male pattern baldness ring visible in the shadows.

Insane blue eyes.

"A question, Lord Wraith?" Nathaniel piped up, unable to help himself.

"Yes?" the man asked, slightly derailed now.

If a train could be *only sort of* off its tracks.

When he got to rolling, the Russian accent became more prominent, but in everyday conversation, say recruiting over coffee in a shop, it was clear that the man had learned English from someone born in Kent and raised in and around London.

Or maybe he'd just spent critical formative years there, though that would have been before the Berlin Wall went down, which would have been a story in and of itself. Nothing on the web suggested that sort of thing. Son of a Soviet diplomat maybe?

Question for a different day. Every head in here had turned

to look his way. Most of them were borderline hostile, but that was just chickens trying to figure out a new pecking order as Lord Wraith had felt the need to hire a new cybersecurity expert, and Nathaniel had been available reasonably cheap.

And desperate.

Maybe he shouldn't have been so desperate, in retrospect?

"All of the satellites?" Nathaniel asked, mostly to confirm what he'd heard before. "Destroy everything in Low Earth Orbit right now? Everything someone else wants to launch later?"

"That's right," Lord Wraith nodded. "The man who's paying us is losing the billionaire space race, and not happy with that prospect. So he intends to make sure that that other asshole doesn't win. Any of the other assholes."

"By seeding low and medium orbital space with enough ball bearings to cause a cascading chain reaction?" Nathaniel pressed, unable to wrap his head around that level of abject insanity. "He's paying you to create a Kessler?"

"Indeed," Lord Wraith purred. "Is that a problem for you, Moriarty?"

Nathaniel felt himself suddenly on a bullseye as everyone suddenly wondered if he was a spy or a fool.

Think fast.

"Yes, it's a problem," Nathaniel answered, speaking quickly before Lady Nyx did more than kip out one nice hip to rest a hand on a pistol. "I own stock in a lot of those companies and need to liquidate my positions if they're all going to be worthless soon."

Blinks back at him. Confusion.

Not a spy. A capitalist. Not *as much* of an enemy, but Nathaniel had a feeling that he'd just moved himself into the unenviable position of a *Kulak* with some of these old

Soviet punks. A rich, middle-class farmer when so many of the peasants had been starving. Stalin had finished them off pretty early and earned himself a lot of credit.

Of course, the Georgian dipshit then pissed it all away pretty quickly after that, but that was the risk one took in being as crazy as a shithouse rat.

Like Lord Wraith.

"I would get into something extremely liquid, Moriarty," Lord Wraith opined intellectually. "When we do this, everything will collapse for a bit. Not entirely terminal, but the current infrastructure of this planet can't handle the loss of all that hardware for the next ten to twenty years. It will be utter chaos, in the best possible way."

Nathaniel forced himself to laugh heartily with the rest of the people around him. To dig deep and put an insane scowl in his eyes at the prospect of crashing *everyone* and **everything**.

Nathaniel didn't know how Lord Wraith was going to do…whatever. Or when.

Why was as clear as the dyed hair on his chin. Crazy as a shithouse rat.

Right now, Nathaniel needed to get out of this room alive.

Then run like hell.

Then find some help.

CHAPTER
ONE

JAKE LIFTED the binoculars and studied the warehouse in the distance as the sun was just about to finally go down.

Los Angeles evening. Skies burning orange already and turning red. Night soon.

Generic industrial area. Bland. One of a long series of anonymous buildings running for miles down the highway from here to Orange County. Older place. Red brick that had survived however many earthquakes over the decades. Might have been a place in the sixties where kids with dreams built hotrod cars.

Jake didn't like operating in Southern California, but this case had required it. Worse, it wasn't one of the regional Mexican gangs causing trouble this time but a group with third-tier links to the Russian government, near as Spencer had been able to determine from his digging and contacts.

That bumbling fool in the White House had spent his entire career telling people he was the greatest businessman and wheeler-dealer in history and at this point seemed to believe his own press releases. That, in spite of the amazing number of bankruptcies the man had managed to inflict on other people. And the law suits for everything and anything that he'd lost so many times.

Jake wouldn't call the man a racist punk to his face, but that was just because there was no way in hell he'd ever be in the same room with that obnoxious son of a bitch. Even for money.

Right now, he felt like a grown-up chasing a giggling toddler who had a full diaper. Nothing he'd ever had to do himself, but it fit the situation. The Russians were pissed at the world and had quietly started escalating things.

Cyberattacks were off the charts these days, but Pacific Force didn't deal with that sort of thing. Jake—or more accurately Spencer—had friends he would call when Jake needed something done along those lines. Folks they'd known in high school or college.

Seattle was filled with nerds who had made a killing by being into computers early on. Some of them had been over in Redmond in the eighties and nineties, then walked away at the top. Jake and his friends had still been in high school but had managed to sell a computer game they had programmed.

Better, done it eighteen years ago in February 2000 just before the dot bomb had turned all those early dreams of wealth to dew and dust for so many people. Hollyanne had wisely convinced him and everyone else to take cash instead of stock options.

Her family traced back to Ahmad Shah Qajar, the last Shah of Iran before the Pahlavi usurpers. The last ruling member of the old Qajar dynasty. All of her immediate family had gotten out of Iran after 1979, many eventually settling in the US and keeping a low profile. They'd carried gold and jewels with them in suitcases. That was the only reason they had money today. They understood such things.

And taking cash up front had been the smartest thing Jake had ever done. How many people could retire at seventeen with fifteen million dollars in the bank? The other four had all done well on their smaller shares. Each of them had looked around as the dotcom exploded and the tides of money suddenly receded in a nasty recession. They'd been able to sit on their cash and wait.

Only Nathaniel had gotten burned, but he'd been the one to angrily split from the rest of them. Going to do it his own way. Eight months later, there'd been no money for the game he'd created. Nothing. He'd managed a scholarship into college but hadn't stayed with it long.

Even then, he'd been so angry at Jake and the gang that he'd gone dark. Criminal. Evil, though always within limits.

Pacific Force had been the answer to Nathaniel's acts. Fifteen years on, the five of them were still at it, though smarter these days. Growing up, maybe.

Forty would be here soon enough.

But right now, thirty-five meant that Jake was at the top of his game physically as well as mentally. And little birdies with federal badges had asked him to meet for coffee up in Seattle and whispered things in his ear. Things that they didn't trust their own political appointee superiors to deal with.

Especially not considering that a lot of folks openly wondered if the President was a Russian agent.

Stooge was obvious. Hopefully that moron didn't destroy the entire United States government before they pried his fingers off the levers of power.

Tomorrow.

Today, Jake had to deal with some Russian *businessmen*.

"How's it look?" Rik asked as she stepped close.

Jake glanced over and did a triple-take.

She hated the name Erika. Hated everything girlie that her parents had ever tried to get her to be as a kid, instead working on being as redneck as she could manage. Bow-hunting, fishing, camping, rebuilding cars, building mechanical toys.

Then today she got dressed up and made Jake's jaw drop.

One-quarter Japanese and three-quarters Anglo-German, where all the genes had lined up perfectly.

Five-foot-eleven with a hint of her Japanese War Bride grandmother in her facial bones and a big chest that balanced nice hips. Gorgeous normally, and now somebody had taken the time to do her in a makeup she rarely wore. Probably both Hollyanne and Grant since he was an expert on seducing people.

Rik was in a low-cut blue top that pushed her chest up a little. Distractingly.

Shoulder-length blonde hair so fine that it was almost invisible on her arms.

"Wow," Jake said. Then wolf-whistled at her, just to get a blush.

And punche in the shoulder.

"Stop it," she growled, still blushing.

"Ready for this? he asked.

"*Я здесь, чтобы поговорить об оружии,*" Rik replied without a hint of an accent. And a twinkle in her eyes.

Finding out that she'd learned Russian at some point had made a lot of his current work much easier. She could pass for Siberian or North Russian easily. Useful today.

She reached into the pocket of her slacks and pulled out an earpiece, handing it to him.

"Spencer and I have been playing with the programming on these," she said. "It should pick up everything down to a whisper, then blank hard on loud noises like gunshots."

"Not supposed to be any gunfire today," Jake reminded her as he tucked it into his right ear. "This is just a meeting to review their merchandise and confirm what they've got for sale so we can arrange something much bigger and let the DEA or whoever have them."

"I'm still armed," Rik said, turning deadly serious in an instant. "So are you. Hollyanne is ready to slip in the side with Grant. Spencer has a couple of surveillance cameras set up and 911 on speed dial. Plus, you don't trust these punks any more than I do, Jake."

He nodded.

Arms dealing with newcomers was always risky. Folks who had been in the business for a while developed trust over time. These men were Chechen punks who probably had knocked over some banks somewhere for seed money. Assuming that they hadn't just gotten a money order from Moscow or Vladivostok to go into business in the States.

Nobody had been able to pierce their organization yet to be certain.

And yes, he was armed. Rik had a friend down in Tacoma who had done most of the gunsmithing. Jake had finally been talked into giving up the old Colt Mustang he'd loved and instead trade up to a Sig Sauer P238 Legion. Still .380, but smoother. And heavily massaged by that same expert. Plus, Jake was loaded with two silver-tipped Glaser Safety Slugs, then an armor-piercing round designed to go through a Class III vest with a titanium heart plate, then four more silver-tips.

If he really had to actually shoot someone, Jake wanted them down fast and hard. It was a rare occurrence, because usually he was able to out-think his opponents. That wasn't the same as being unprepared. Hopefully, he wouldn't need it today.

The Sig was a sub-compact, so it holstered well on his right kidney, the old FBI carry.

He checked it now, drawing the slide back just enough to confirm one in the chamber. Rik nodded.

"Testing audio," Jake said.

"Clear signal," Spencer replied immediately.

"Also testing," Rik said.

"Got you both."

"This is Hollyanne. I'm in position."

"Grant here. I've got her flank."

"I hear you all fine," Spencer said. "Whenever you're ready, Jake."

Jake nodded to Rik.

All his nice cars, the ones she worked on and improved, were still back in Seattle in the garage. Instead, Grant had borrowed an armored SUV from a diplomat friend here in LA, swapping the plates out for something he had apparently stolen off a Corvette in a parking lot somewhere.

Probably somebody who had been an asshole to him in the store, knowing Grant. Corvette drivers these days tended to fall into a pretty narrow demographic. Jake didn't ask.

Instead, he moved to the driver's seat. Rik got into the back. It was her show today, with him as her driver and punk bodyguard.

And the rest of Pacific Force backing them up.

CHAPTER
TWO

HOLLYANNE WATCHED the building and contemplated the nature of evil. You destroy it, rather than coddling such a thing in the hopes that it might seek redemption later. Not everyone saw things that starkly, but she'd spent too much time watching what evil did under the assumed disguise of innocence.

The assholes over there were happy to sell modern military hardware to anyone with cash, something Los Angeles and the rest of the world didn't really need. She couldn't save the world, but she could help Jake take these fools down.

Hard.

She was dressed today like something of a ninja. Not the all-black of television, but the low-profile nobodies that they had been in the real world, where their job had been to infiltrate a target secretly, get close to the target, and kill them anonymously.

Not that she was expecting to get to that level tonight, but it was a mindset.

Baggy gray gi-pants that gathered at the ankles. Three-quarter-top trainers on her feet. Blue shirt dark enough to fade into the background over a sports bra made with enough kevlar to turn a knife in close. She'd left the rest of the gi at the hotel and worn a blue, denim jacket she'd originally bought in Aberdeen a few years ago. It was still her favorite.

Compact Sig .380 on one hip, but she'd reach for her baton first, stored on her right thigh and ready to snap out into four feet of steel tube.

Night was falling. Jake and Rik were in the truck. She turned to Grant.

"It won't be pretty," she reminded him.

"If they were nicer people, I could have probably run some excellent con job on them and saved us all this mess," he shrugged. "If they gotta go down, they made that decision when they got out of bed this morning. Nobody made them come down here."

Hollyanne nodded. Grant was a social chameleon. A con artist who used his powers for good. Mostly. A smiling face who could seduce anybody into any manner of silliness if needed.

Not her taste in bed, but not bad. Just a little too shallow most of the time. A pretty face who didn't have much behind it.

Except that he'd also turned a little more philosophical in the two years Pacific Force had been mostly retired. Like now.

Hollyanne put a hand on her holster to confirm it, then on the baton. Grant went ahead and drew his pistol, mostly because he wasn't fast with a gun. His job was covering her ass anyway, rather than expecting to confront anyone.

"Let's go," she said. "Spencer, team two in motion."

"Copy that."

Hollyanne slipped one eyeball around the side of the building and confirmed that there was nobody in sight over there. No windows on this side of the building. No cameras that Spencer had been able to spot.

Should be blind. Jake would drive to the front where there was a garage door and a small office like an old service station. The back had a porch where folks could sit and smoke in the old days.

Nobody visible, so she moved, crossing diagonally then sliding along the wall, eyes all directions including up for cameras, but Jake would have mentioned it if he'd seen someone on the roof. Grant slipped along behind her, exceptionally quiet for a guy who didn't do this much.

He had her back. She moved to the next corner and peeked around. The door was open to catch whatever breeze might be coming off the distant water, but things were still tonight. Smelled like sand, salt, ozone, and hot grease from a fish and chips shack two blocks over. Wouldn't cool down for a few hours, then it would be colder than crap by morning.

"Rear door appears open," she said just loud enough for everyone on the circuit to hear.

"Copy that," Jake replied. "Approaching now."

She could hear the truck grinding closer over hot asphalt roads a little thick with blown sand and dirt. They made a much different sound than you got almost anywhere else. Seattle had enough rain that the crap would wash away and you'd get squeaks.

There were lights on inside, but no shadows at the door, so she checked up. No cameras outside here, either. Maybe none, but never assume that.

She was facing off with paranoid, confrontational punks who had ready access to heavy firepower.

Hollyanne motioned Grant around the corner, where he trailed her by several steps as she moved to the back side of the door and peeked into the gap between door and frame.

The inside was a mess of old metal racks on the back half, with crap stacked on them and next to them. The smell of old rust and thick grease was evident now. Probably stuff that had been here since that big aerospace recession ripped through Southern California in the early nineties.

There were several men in the open space closer to the garage door space. All of them armed with at least a pistol. A few had big, black assault rifles. Russian make. Probably Russian Army issue, though she was dead certain that they'd show up stolen if anybody were to trace the serial numbers.

Might have even been legitimately stolen. The group all looked like punks. Hard and unshaven. Cauliflower ears and broken noses. Probably hadn't showered today. Russian issue troops. Little green men, to use one common insult.

None were looking her way, because the far side the garage door was opening with a rattle of chains and ungreased wheels. Hollyanne slipped around the back door and put her butt against the wall on the far side. No easy way to watch, but she could listen. Being on this side meant that she could react quickly.

Grant took her spot at the crack of the door.

"Jake just pulled up and into the garage," he whispered a running commentary. "I have eyes-on and Hollyanne can react quickly. He's pulled to a stop and shut down the motor. Four men, heavily armed, joking in Russian. Several crates of weapons labeled in Cyrillic stacked to one side, with one of them open. Jake and Rik, we've got your back. You're on."

CHAPTER
THREE

NATHANIEL'S JOB was to handle all things cybersecurity for the Dark Citizen Movement from his tiny, dark office, but they still weren't entirely trusting him at this point. Not that he could complain much. His own soldier *Lucky* had kept Nathaniel from going right back to an English prison after Jake caught them or being traded to the Americans—or worse—so Nathaniel had had to take whatever gig he could find.

Old contact of an old contact sort of thing. Now he was minioning for a lunatic. Or all of them.

Adding insult to injury, as it were.

The woman across the desk from him had set up the original electronic perimeter around Lord Wraith. And she'd been pretty good at what she did. Not world-class, like Nathaniel liked to think of himself on a good day, but adequate to deal with average governments and keep North Korean, Chinese, and Russian hacking attempts mostly at bay.

It helped that Dark Citizen didn't need a lot of visibility on the internet. Exactly the opposite, if anything. Twenty-First Century Survivalists, lurking in the shadows as much as humanly possible without needing to expose websites or server back ends to the insanity of all the bored and dangerous script kiddies out there. Grandkids of those weirdos from the 1980s. Or renegade Mormons. You could never be too sure.

Just another kind of cult, but this one might be dangerous enough to actually be a problem.

All his adult life, Nathaniel had been a criminal. Raging against Jake and the gang. Then against the world.

Raging against the machine.

There were, however, lines he did not cross. Ever. Families were off-limits, his and theirs. That included Mrs. Johnson who was Jake's housekeeper in Seattle, as well as any musical acts she had invited to use the recording studio out back. Whoever they were.

Nathaniel just wanted to get rich. To be generally acknowledged as the mastermind that he was.

Hard to do that if some idiot decided to crash the global economy, end the modern world, and overthrow however many governments were going to go down with it. Might be most of them that mattered, considering how tightly intertwined everything was electronically these days.

That would be bad.

And there wasn't much he could do about them not trusting him much yet. Lord Wraith, at least, and that man had instructed the woman sitting across from him to be extra watchful over anything he did. That included all his old email accounts and various websites that he owned, however many layers of corporate obfuscation deep Nathaniel was. They were all set to auto-update, so things stayed out as close to the edge of secured as he could keep them. That was just smart, since he could not talk to them right now.

Instead, he studied the woman who was his assistant. Whose job he had largely taken over, causing her to be demoted. If you wanted to look at it that way. She seemed to be handling it well, but he'd also come in and taken a lot of things up an entire level from what she'd managed, and she seemed smart enough to understand that.

Her name was *Gothic Chip*. Why, Nathaniel had no idea. Nor did he really care, other than to confirm early on that she'd come from Portland, Oregon originally, where steampunk had buried itself so deeply in the fandom's cultural DNA as to be endemic these days.

Brown. Stood out, when so many of the others wore either all black or some bold, primary color with black highlights. Not her.

GC had no name she'd been willing to share with him. But she only knew him as Moriarty unless she'd been smart enough to run him through a face match algorithm. And she probably was.

They were alone in his office with the door closed, though that was professional, and not personal. The woman was too old for him, being somewhere on the far side of fifty. And not the well-preserved kind that made you stop and ogle as she walked by. No, overweight and stuffed into a too-small corset that should have been retied at some point. Looked painful and she wheezed when the room was perfectly quiet.

Like now.

Brown hair, but that was a cheap home dye job. Pancake makeup too heavy on skin with acne scars. Makeup drawn around the eyes like kohl to make them more elongated and possibly stylish. At least on another woman. Brown eyes. Brown corset. Brown leather shoulder piece with gorget around her neck. Brown cotton skirt over brown leggings. Brown lace-up boots.

It would have helped if everything was either closer in color or more contrasting, but no, everything was just off enough to be *wrong*.

At least she was smart, if something of an emotional descendant of the Baader–Meinhof Group/Red Army Faction lunatics that had been destructive anarchists in West Germany before Nathaniel's time. Way before his time.

He didn't think she'd been one of them. Probably too young, unless she was a niece or groupie who came along after folks had finally started cracking down on that shit.

He suppressed the shiver. Those people had been the wrong kind of criminal. Crazy and destructive for the sake of blowing shit up.

What Lord Wraith seemed to be aspiring to.

He'd been watching the woman. She was watching him. He gave up trying to outstubborn her.

"I need to contact the outside world," Nathaniel said abruptly. "You heard Lord Wraith talk. I'd like to get to my various brokers and liquidate things quietly into gold or maybe Euros before I'm flat broke."

"How many brokers do you have?" she asked with a furrowed brow.

Smart, but not worldly. Ivory tower intellectual, though probably still cinder blocks in her case. Lady Nyx at least had brains and a cosmopolitan sophistication. GC was a steampunk goth who knew computers.

"Let's see," Nathaniel mused, leaning back and staring at a spot over her shoulder where the paint job had been half-assed at some point. He could see the mustard cream underneath the current gray of the walls. "New York. Hong Kong. Tokyo. Berlin. London. Shanghai. Seattle. And Cleveland."

"Cleveland?" she asked. "Why the hell Cleveland?"

"Because you asked that question," he smiled. "Always fly below the radar until they force you up. Safer that way. Lord Wraith and the others keep things quiet. A broker in Cleveland is nobody who folks looking for me would expect because I have absolutely no connections to the city."

She blinked too many times, like a cow with an especially tasty cud trying to solve trigonometric functions. Which was rude, but she'd done little to convince him to take her seriously on anything but a purely technical level.

GC was a decidedly intelligent woman. Nowhere near sneaky enough to impress him.

"Why so many?" she demanded, finally latching on to the pure incoherence of the concept.

"Most of them aren't in my birth name," he replied, holding the sneer inside but just shadowing his tones with it. "Various passports and identities I've created or acquired over the years so that I could hide from my enemies."

"So how will you contact everyone?" Brow still furrowed. Probably the mind behind it, too.

"I have memorized everything I need," Nathaniel replied, softening his anger at being questioned.

It was all reflexive paranoia on their part, rather than anything he'd done. Lord Wraith would have had someone shoot him in the back of the head if they had any reason at all.

"So what do you need then?" GC asked.

"Considering how delicate things are around here, what I would like is for someone to hit a pawn shop or something around here and pick me up a used laptop that's been flattened and rebuilt," Nathaniel replied. "Preferably a basic Windows machine, though I could make do with a Chromebook if I had to. That, or buy it used and then let me flatten it here inside a Faraday cage. Really, what I need is a clean device that exists solely to let me onto the internet anonymously. Then someone can drive me to an internet cafe or coffee shop with an open wi-fi node that I can use. We don't dare send any sorts of signals out from these machines here in the warehouse, because of the risk that someone might track it back to us. This way, I've completely anonymized myself. Best they could do is track me to an IP address, which maybe gets them to a city, but as soon as I'm done, we'll put the machine in a press and utterly destroy it so that nobody can ever trace it or use it as evidence."

He didn't say that it would be Lord Wraith or one of his other minions finding evidence that Nathaniel was betraying them. Again, bullets in his head. Maybe while he slept.

No thank you very much.

"That's it?" she asked.

From the confusion in her eyes, she was still trying to calculate how he might be betraying them. **Not** opening their network wasn't a scenario they had gamed out, obviously. Whatever else they had planned.

But he was the new guy. He understood that trust had to be built over time.

"That's it," Nathaniel confirmed. "Talk to Lord Wraith and see if he'll sign off on it. If so, somebody needs to find me a machine that is raw OS with no current updates. I won't let it do anything while I'm connected, then we shut it down, bring it home, and burn it. Safest way to talk to the outside world once. Like I said, I'd rather not be broke when all this goes down, so I figure I need to do it sooner rather than later."

"Oh, you've got about five weeks," she nodded nonchalantly.

Nathaniel had engaged in high-stakes negotiations with some incredibly dangerous men and women in his time. The folks who had a gun on their side of the table and a willingness to shoot you in the face if they thought they needed to.

As a result, he had developed a poker face so smooth that butter wouldn't melt in his mouth. Right now, he needed it. Nathaniel was pure innocence as her eyes got huge.

Operational Security breach. The kind that might get her killed if he wanted to say something to someone who might take offense that he knew.

Nathaniel played it casual.

"Long as I've got a week, it's good," he continued, as if she hadn't said anything meaningful. "Tomorrow is Thursday. If I can send my messages out then, they might be able to start liquidating my various positions Friday, but it's more likely that they'll do things in small chunks, so I don't figure the last set of sell orders will go out until next Wednesday. Won't finalize until Thursday. A week from today I am hopefully entirely liquid, though if I thought it would matter, I might exercise a massive number of options for the drop. Not going to help if there's nobody around to close them next year, ya know?"

"Ain't that the truth," she agreed.

From the look in her eyes, GC was hoping he hadn't understood the significance of five weeks.

Now, he just had to find a way to get out of this mess, bring in some help, and maybe save the world.

Shit, he hated that idea. Who the hell would believe a guy like him?

Fortunately, he knew one person who would.

RIK WAS grumpy about having to be dressed like a businesswoman bimbo but didn't let it reach her eyes. Hollyanne liked to tease her occasionally about being bikini bait, and Rik worked her ass off to stay slinky. Much harder than the little Persian Princess, but she got to tease Hollyanne about that.

Today, the damned bra was pinching and squishing. By design, sure, but still a pain in the ass. And other places. The pistol on the belt in front, underneath where her top blossomed out, didn't help.

Given her choice, she'd have been the sniper on this one, standing off on overwatch with a rifle or a bow to lend support or superior firepower.

But these mooks needed to be distracted. She kept glancing down, expecting to be spilling over the top.

Jake pulled to a stop and shut the truck down. He slipped out, then opened her door.

Rik could have gone for heels to make her look taller than everyone present but she hated balancing on stilts, so she'd gone with some sensible flats. Better than her Chuckie-T's, though not as comfortable. Designer blue jeans that went on forever. Blue blouse with a darker jacket over it, everything arranged in Vees to focus the eyes down and center. Boobs. Blond hair loose and brushed back.

She moved out from behind the door and watched jaws fall open and tongues hang out. She'd owe Jake a quarter after this. Damn it, she hated losing bets.

"Good afternoon," she said warmly in Russian to the man who looked like he was in charge. "You are Boris?"

"I am," he replied in the same tongue. "You are Ekaterina?"

"Yes," she said languidly, stretching everything and pressing her chest forward a little as she moved towards them.

Jake practically vanished into her shadow.

By design.

"What exciting *surprises* do you boys have for me?" Rik asked as she stopped just out of arm's reach from Boris.

Tantalizingly close.

Rik was always shocked senseless when it worked.

She wasn't the pretty one. Hollyanne was.

But Persian was not right for this scene, since the dealers looked Chechen.

All around her, brains reset. Tongues got dry then withdrawn before too much drool spilled. Four men stared at her chest like they saw Aphrodite emerging from the waves.

Rik turned serious. Focused herself on Boris. The man qualied a little under her gaze.

Then he managed to focus his eyes up high enough to ignore her chest and look at her face.

"Guns?" she asked, sharpening her tone.

"Yes," he managed, finally breaking free of whatever spell her boobs had cast on him. Maybe. "Come."

He gestured and she followed him over, reading the side of the box.

"Zima rifles," Boris announced proudly. "ZKN-15."

"Oh," Rik tried not to sound too disappointed. Much. "Not the 12? Something chambered in 7.62×39mm is going to be difficult to sell around here, unless you've got fifteen or twenty pallets of ammunition somewhere handy at a good price. 5.45×39mm tends to be more common in the United States after so many decades of importing it for the American civilian market."

Rik looked around but didn't see anything like that with the stuff in sight. Just eight wooden crates of the ZKN-15. Boris looked a little crestfallen. His men had shellshocked faces.

Probably not used to a woman who could discuss Russian military ballistics casually.

Oh, buttercup…

"Still, let's see what you've got and if it might be *enough* for a girl like me," she smiled, taking the sting out of the previous rebuke. And to set minds racing again with the double *entendre*.

The crate was open, with several rifles stacked and a few pulled out. The three peons had identical weapons either in hand or on straps hanging barrel down. Presumably all loaded. Boris only had a pistol.

Rik pulled the farthest one from the crate and lifted it. Not bad. Russians did fantastic engineering design when it came to killing people. It was the shoddy workmanship in the factories you had to pay attention to.

These were all so new that they might be stuff developed for front line troops. Or factory leftovers dumped on the open market when the Russian Army refused to accept them.

She turned to the nearest punk with a rifle. The only one holding his instead of having it slung on his shoulder.

"Give me your magazine," she ordered with a snap of her fingers. "I want to see how it moves."

The man paused, glancing at Boris, but got the nod he needed and popped out his magazine, handing it to her.

Thirty rounds. Presumably down one knowing punks like these. Rik put the stock on her hip and slammed the magazine home. The slide to chamber a round worked a lot like an old HK33 she had in her arms locker back home. Handle that pivoted out to give you a good hold when it latched. You popped it with your left hand and let it do all the work.

She wondered if whoever designed these had copied a HK mechanism for this. You should always steal from quality work, after all. And it moved well for something expected to be new-in-box and still getting all the packing grease knocked loose. Good weapons always took a bit to settle in.

Still, Rik had what she needed. Real guns and not factory rejects. Likely stolen, but Spencer could always track them down for someone once they were no longer a threat to spill out onto the streets for some lunatic with a chip on his shoulder and politicians edging ever closer to inciting a civil war.

All four men were in front of her now. She had the safety on and the weapon pointed straight up. Finger outside the well.

She caught Grant's eyes through the crack of the door and smiled.

"Yes," she announced with a smile. "This is exactly the sort of thing we might need in order to throw a party around here. How many more do you have if my buyers decide that these crates aren't enough?"

She'd ended up smiling at Boris. Just because, Rik pulled her shoulders slowly back as she drew a breath. Stupid, but it worked.

Men.

Throw a party had been the code that Hollyanne needed. She slipped in the back door like a ghost, eyeballing everything and pulling out that nasty telescoping baton she liked when she wanted to get close.

"This is all we have currently in stock," Boris hesitated. "But I can make a few calls and get more put on a boat from Vladivostok this afternoon. From there to Hong Kong to shuffle things around then they'll cross the Pacific. Six to eight weeks delivery."

Rik cocked her head to one side, as if considering it. He'd really answered the only question she had. Jake's concern had been a storage unit, here or down in Orange County, where failure to pay rent meant that the contents would be auctioned off. Or simply stolen in this case, considering the street value in California.

"The price for this shipment is good," she nodded. "I'll talk to my buyers and call you tomorrow."

Rik took a step forward, putting her even with Boris and causing the man to turn in place to follow her. One more step and she suddenly lunged forward and used the butt of her rifle to hit the goon on the left in the stomach as hard as she could.

He went down.

Hollyanne came out of the shadows and took the one on the right down with a sound like a bag of potatoes spilling.

The last goon, the one in the middle, pointed his rifle at her and pulled the trigger with a loud click.

"ZKN-15 won't fire without a magazine inserted," she reminded him with a smile.

Then punched him in the face, knocking him on his ass.

"No," Jake said over the sudden silence.

Rik looked back and Jake had his pistol pointed in Boris's face from close enough that the tiny .380 barrel probably looked like a shotgun's bore.

Boris stopped moving and took his hands off his pistol slowly, putting his hands in the air.

"You are under arrest," Jake smiled.

Rik flipped her own safety off now and covered the three gasping and puking on the floor, just in case any of them felt feisty. Hollyanne stripped weapons and tossed them into a corner. Grant appeared at the door and stepped in to collect things.

"Who are you people?" Boris asked, shocked into a rasp.

"We're Pacific Force," Rik smiled at him.

CHAPTER
FIVE

NATHANIEL CARRIED himself with the sort of carefree *bonhomie* that you usually only saw in movies when a character knew they had script immunity from whatever stupid shit was about to happen to everyone else. It was bullshit, but he had a role to play, and if he fucked this up, he was dead meat cooling by the side of the road before nightfall anyway.

It helped that Bonn was lovely today. All of Germany was having one of those late spring/early summer days that filled poets and musicians with dreams of love. Or whatever it was they did when they went on to write happy things still quoted long after they were dead.

Nathaniel was on foot, with a new laptop in an old messenger bag over his shoulder and occasionally banging on his right hip as he walked.

Lady Nyx—named for the Goddess of Night he presumed though he had never worked up the curiosity to ask—walked along his left side, holding hands with him like this was some sort of date. Nathaniel assumed that she was there to make sure he didn't bolt.

She was dressed casually. Touristy, so she fit in, in jeans and a black T-shirt for a band Nathaniel didn't know. Like him, she had a thing on her outer hip that was a large purse or small messenger bag, but hers didn't have a computer in it.

His guess was at least one of her signature pistols and probably a couple of flash/bang stun grenades. Maybe a smoker, too.

She had impressed him as a woman prepared to escalate any dangerous situation immediately to extremely stupid levels, but Nathaniel supposed that such an attitude was necessary when you were a terrorist. And all the rest of them were terrorists, as near as he could tell.

Different shine to the eyes from a mere criminal like him. Far greater emotional and psychological commitment to something big. Usually an *-ism* of some sort. They were all bad when you took them too far.

Today, she was pretending to be *Amanda*, while he was being *Dave*. Not like it mattered much except in whatever polite conversation they might engage in while sipping coffee as he connected to the outer world and contacted all his brokers. Two English tourists in town. The only person who might remember that name later would be the barista on the other side of the counter, after all.

But he could smile and pretend this was a date with a pretty girl. Right up until she shot him in the back of the head. Nathaniel wouldn't have much choice in the matter.

The shop itself was quiet, in that weird, mid-morning moment when all the first wave of folks had gone to work and the late sleepers had not quite roused to face the glorious day. He'd flipped a coin about coming in when it was super busy, but that just meant more people possibly walking by his table and reading over his shoulder as he typed.

Best not.

So he walked to the counter with his pretty date and ordered. Biggest coffee chain in the world, so utterly predictable. He might even drink some, but they believed that tar scraped off the road outside the shop was too under-roasted for them want to actually make coffee from it.

Amanda did the same. *Dave* paid with cash he'd been given as part of this cover, then led them to a corner where he could work without interruption because of a wall behind him. Laptop came out and he got to work. Amanda kept watch like a starved hawk promised fresh rabbit.

Nathaniel ran power to the socket because the machine was going to take a while as it configured itself for the very first time and demanded that he log in with an existing email account so that they could trace him wherever he went in the world.

Winston Smith was supposed to have been a warning, once upon a time, about allowing the government too much control over people's lives. *1984*. Instead, they had off-loaded all the work to a dozen megacorporations and then occasionally walked in a side door demanding electronic records. Sometimes, they even had warrants when they did it, but such a thing was rare, according to Nathaniel's contacts back in that world.

Just badges and attitudes.

Bullies with guns.

Amanda got his coffee when it came up and smiled as she handed it to him.

"Thank you," he said simply, looking up and appreciating her.

GC would have been gruff at best and probably completely bitchy, mostly because she'd have had to dress in normal clothing to come outside the warehouse compound that Lord Wraith had *acquired* at some point.

"So how did you end up in this gig?" she asked innocently as she sat again. "Last I'd heard, your people were in Birmingham being naughty."

Nathaniel went cold all over. He forced himself to finish typing the sentence he was in the middle of, then looked carefully at the woman.

She was not holding a pistol. Didn't even have a hand in her bag like she was about to shoot him dead right here in the store.

"Birmingham?" he asked delicately.

Not quite pretending a faux innocence, but perhaps to clarify that he'd heard her correctly the first time.

"That's right," she grinned at him, then sipped her delicate, floofy whatever-it-was she'd gotten.

The kind that would look like a *bingo* at a regular shop, with every box down the side checked.

"Luck, I suppose you could call it," Nathaniel replied.

Again, not evasion so much as leaving out details that innocent bystanders at other tables might be able to piece together later.

And Lucky—aka one Sokoro Otieno, which came out of Swahili as '*The Lucky One*'—had managed to escape his shackles, overpower a guard, then get the two of them to freedom and safety.

To be extra safe, Lucky had returned to Kenya for a time—going to ground as it were—while Nathaniel had ended up in Germany.

"Good or bad?" Lady Nix asked.

Nathaniel held up his hands like a balance and wavered them back and forth.

"Good," he said. "Right up until Pacific Force came

out of retirement to chase me. Bad at that point. Good later when it got me here."

After all, how many guys got paid to sit in coffee shops talking to pretty women?

"Pacific Force?" she gasped quietly.

"My old pal Jake is still as good as he ever was," Nathaniel offered. Not *quite* rubbing it in that the good guys had still required the very best to catch him but alluding to it.

Lord Wraith talked a good game, but he wasn't playing in the Premier League these days. This whatever-he-had-planned was supposed to catapult him into the top levels of criminal nobility.

At least for as long as such a distinction held any meaning if you were going to crash most of the world's economies.

Hard to be impressive if you suddenly kill a lot of people because food deliveries and supply ships get lost, isn't it?

"What's he like?" she asked now. "Jake."

Nathaniel couldn't tell if she was turned on or clinically nailing down all the details she might need to kill the man later. A little of both, from the flush on her cheeks and the way her pupils dilated.

"My height," Nathaniel said, going back to typing furiously while he had her distracted. Whatever the distraction might be. "Face is more angular than mine, like something Nagel would have drawn in the 80s. Folks still think we're brothers when we're standing beside each other, if they don't know any better. Whip smart. Good with his hands as well as guns. Expert combat driver. The rest of them are all specialists in their own fields, but Jake's the leader that keeps them focused."

"Are they really that good?" she asked. Again, she wanted to sneer, but might also be panting. Weird, but everyone had their own kinks.

"They are that lucky, Amanda," he said, needing a name to drive it home, even though it wasn't hers. It got through to her. "Patton, I think, always said he'd rather be lucky than good. Jake and gang are both. Never underestimate them. I did, and it cost me. Now I'm working for somebody else, doing a thing, and trying to get by."

"Do you like the new boss?" she asked.

Nathaniel wondered if she was trying to entrap him now. Get him to say something stupid in public so as to trigger a sanction.

A woman like Lady Nix only had one sanction. An ultimate one.

"I respect his vision," Nathaniel countered, turning things a little sideways. And still typing. "Don't know him well enough to like or dislike the man, but he's built something truly impressive. Something like I had planned on doing, had Birmingham not gone pear-shaped on me."

"Oh?" she asked, suddenly WAY MORE ATTENTIVE.

"Yup," Nathaniel nodded, hitting send while her brain was elsewhere, then carefully deleting the message he'd just typed from the sent folder. "That whole job was to make a big splash of money and power so that I could recruit a better breed of folks than the hooligans that had been my base before."

"So you might do something similar later?" she asked.

Suddenly, the woman was leaning towards him. Focused on him in ways that didn't scream 'pistol coming out of her bag imminently.' Smiling. She even licked her lips and bit the bottom one, but that honestly looked unconscious.

More than weird. More turned on? Or was she also having second thoughts about blowing up the world?

It was one thing to hold corporations and governments hostage for money. Something entirely else to just burn the world down.

Not every cop or criminal got that.

"That sort of thing is out of my hands right now," Nathaniel replied carefully. "Things are supposedly well along their way elsewhere. If it all comes together, there might not be any reason or need to strike out on my own and rebuild what I used to have, you know?"

"But you would?" she asked, still a little breathless.

Nathaniel shrugged.

"Not everybody wants to work for someone else," he offered evasively. "But I've got a job to do right now and I'll do it to the best of my ability. After he no longer needs me, I have plans. And access to resources. Not enough to start big again, but I won't be reduced to panhandling."

"Keep my number in your book," she said abruptly, firing a phone number at him. English, from the country code and sequence.

Nathaniel memorized it. She might be on the level. She might be setting him up for Lord Wraith. Maybe she wanted a date with Jake.

This was a weird business, and there was no way he could ask anything even remotely useful without tipping his hand to the woman.

At that point, she'd kiss him or kill him.

Not worth finding out today.

And he wasn't some damned princess in a tower waiting to be rescued by whatever big stud came along.

Nathaniel powered the machine down and threw it in his bag. When he got back to the warehouse, he would haul it into his lab, pull the hard drive, then smash it with a hammer before running it through the biggest electro-magnet he could lay hands on.

Fools were going to destroy the world if somebody didn't stop them.

Why the fuck did it have to be him?

CHAPTER
SIX

JAKE WAS SITTING at the Burgermaster just off the east end of the 520 bridge in Bellevue when his phone chirped. Lunch, but he'd had some meetings with his broker Solomon in town and slipped away rather than walk to one of the nicer joints close by.

A greasy double was calling his name this morning. Or rather had, mostly gone already, along with all of the fries. The inside of his truck would smell nice all day.

He'd taken one of the old beaters today for errands. 1988 Jeep Comanche Pickup in glossy black. Back when pickups were a bench and a bed, rather than the current oversized four-door sedan with an open-topped trunk too small to haul anything useful.

Jake's vehicle collection was compact and precise. Mostly for personal use, rather than hangar queens for show. The cab of the Comanche had been lined with kelvar cloth, for instance.

Just in case.

He answered.

"Spencer," Jake said around the last bite. "What's happening in the world today?"

"You sitting down?" Spencer asked in a nervous voice.

Jake felt a chill run down his spine.

"Should I have a gun in one hand?" he asked in an off-hand way.

"Not yet," Spencer said, deadly serious. "Probably later. I just got a weird-ass email that turned out to be a tip about a wanted criminal, including giving us a time and a date and a location where we might be able to surprise the man and arrest him."

"Okay," Jake prompted.

Things like that happened. The underworld was notorious for turning on each other, given enough time. Bad attitudes and puffed-up egos. Unhealthy mix.

"Here's the best part," Spencer said with a hard, ugly laugh. "It's Nathaniel."

"Somebody actually knows where he is and is setting him up for us?" Jake confirmed.

Again, weird, but not impossible. If you weren't configured for that sort of operation, it was much better to bring in experts. Plus, any government you called was likely to be so full of leaks that the information—and the informant's identity—would get back to a guy like Nathaniel in days, if not hours.

"Worse, Jake," Spencer said. "The email came from Nathaniel himself."

CHAPTER
SEVEN

HOLLYANNE WAS SEATED across the big table from Jake, with Rik on the high side, Spencer on the other end, and Grant next to her. Mrs. Johnson had some friends out in the recording studio tonight, with a stack of pizzas and two-liter bottles of soda just delivered. They would be out there until dawn, doing whatever.

Pacific Force had the main house and privacy for now.

"What do we know?" Jake asked.

They'd only been back from LA for a week now. Just enough time to relax for a couple of days, but not enough to wander too far afield and get into other projects.

"It was a code," Spencer replied. "But one we used to use back in the bad old days when we didn't want any of the teachers reading over our shoulders as we typed. Y'all remember those."

Hollyanne grinned with the rest of them. Jake and Spencer had built the engine itself. Rik had made it look pretty. Hollyanne and Grant had polished their areas of expertise. Close combat and seduction, as it were.

"So it comes across as an order to his broker in Cleveland," Spencer continued, his Armenian ancestry turning even darker with blood as he got worked up. "Cleveland was always a code phrase. Lots of meanings but this one says he is serious. And he embedded other information in the code to let us know where and when he expected to be. Bonn, Germany, of all places, so he didn't really go far when he escaped the British."

"What was the actual message about?" Hollyanne asked now.

Something didn't sit right. Nathaniel knew all their phone numbers. He could have called any one of them, any time he wanted. This felt like he was being held hostage.

Nathaniel Hoestler wouldn't react well to that sort of thing, but Pacific Force was a much nicer rescue than he might have arranged with all his Brighton and Hove hooligans. Maybe more professional? Reliable? Something.

"He's asking me to liquidate all his assets into cash," Spencer replied, turning to face her. "Slowly and quietly, rather than immediately, as long as it is done in a week. Doesn't want to short any stocks, naked or otherwise, but seems convinced that there is a hard market crash coming in the medium term. How far out, I can't tell."

Hollyanne stirred. Felt the grimace twist her features.

"Hollyanne?" Jake asked.

He was in charge, but she was Second-in-Command, if only because the other three tended to fall more into support roles most of the time. She and Jake were the ones that kicked in doors.

"If he was engineering a thing, he'd be trying to corner the market. Naked stock shorts and exactly that sort of thing."

"Naked?" Rik asked, confused.

"You borrow stock from somebody who owns it," Grant piped up. "Sell it at today's price, with an understanding that you will buy it back and return it later. If the stock goes down, you pocket the difference as profit. If it goes up, you lose. And can lose however much it takes to make somebody else whole. Usually, options to buy at a certain price are safer, because you pay a small fee up front for them, but aren't required to actually do anything on that date if the price goes the wrong way. Like say, the stock is forty today, but you buy options to get it at thirty-six in a month. But something happens and a month from now it is around thirty. You ignore the option and buy on the open market. But if it goes to fifty, you can get rich."

"So he's not manipulating the market," Rik nodded. "Not obviously, anyway."

"Yeah," Hollyanne agreed. "He knows that something is going to happen. Might even know when. Wants to have only cash in hand on that day. That suggests that someone else is doing something bad. So bad that it won't recover later, but he doesn't want to tip his hand."

"He also wants us to kidnap or capture him," Jake said.

"Or rescue him?" Hollyanne asked.

All eyes snapped around.

"He's doing something out of character," she tapped fingers down to count on the tabletop. "He's invoked Cleveland to let Spencer know that this is supposedly not a drill or a taunt. He's telling us that something bad is coming, but he's not in a position to say what or when. I read that as somebody watching over his shoulder, like Mrs. Craig used to in the computer lab."

"He's asking us for help?" Rik scoffed. "That shit?"

"He knows that nobody else would listen," Jake chimed in. "No government is going to take a call from Nathaniel Hoestler that doesn't involve them sending special forces assault teams after him. Or calling someone else who can."

"What are we?" Hollyanne asked, grinning. "Chopped liver?"

"We don't shoot first, last I checked," Jake grinned back. "Sometimes, punch them in the gob and get them to all surrender nicely. It happens. FBI or DEA or whoever would have kicked in the door and opened fire full auto, down in LA, and you know it."

Hollyanne felt the grimace return.

"Nathaniel needs help," she said, unbelieving. "Needs us because he can't think of anybody else who would answer. How bad has it gotten? Whatever *it* is."

"That bad," Jake nodded. "It might be a trap. That's always a risk in this business. But we have two weeks to his strike date to drive up and disappear him. Assume we don't bring in the Germans, NATO, or anybody else, because they'll leak. Or jump the gun and force Nathaniel to scrub when he sees unfamiliar faces around. I don't have answers immediately. What I have are questions. Do we believe him? Do we rescue him? Do we go now and try to hide in Bonn, not knowing who might recognize us? Or do we wait here then move at the last minute? You think on that. I'd like to take the afternoon and just let it roll around in the back of my head. Let's meet up again for dinner. I can cook or we can go somewhere quiet."

"Ask Carrie to come cook, if she's available?" Rik asked. "That keeps our conversation private and she can just throw it in the oven early with instructions so simple even you can follow them."

Hollyanne grinned as Jake blushed. But the woman was a professional at-home kind of chef for folks who didn't want someone full-time, but didn't always want to cook.

"I'll call her," Jake nodded. "If she's busy, you get my cooking and you'll like it."

They all laughed. Everyone liked to tease one another, and Jake was actually good in the kitchen.

"Okay, see you in a couple of hours, then," he said, rising.

Hollyanne did the same.

Some of this just didn't fit right. But it was Nathaniel.

To survive the criminal underworld for as long as he had, he had to be sneaky and dangerous.

Had he finally run into someone nastier than him?

CHAPTER
EIGHT

JAKE'S RIDE today was the old 1939 Plymouth/1940 Chevy front/back hackjob in electric purple that was Rik's favorite rebuild. Thoroughly modern underneath the skin. Desperately overpowered, even for the wide tires in back. Mostly bulletproof.

Stupid fast but handled like a gazelle.

Hollyanne was riding in the passenger seat, five-point harness on, just in case. Jake wore the same.

You never expected trouble, but it rarely called ahead and made a reservation.

Errands. Nothing important or critical. All things he could have logged in, ordered, and had delivered to the massive mansion he had inherited from his parents.

Slippery-easy way to never leave the house again.

So he drove.

"You are amazingly quiet," he noted as they bombed past I-90, headed south towards Newcastle and Renton.

"Nathaniel is asking us to trust him," she replied, about the time Jake figured she'd ignored him.

"He is," Jake nodded. Traffic was not bad right now, so

they were actually moving, instead of idling along in the long parking lot you got most of the day on 405. And a good chunk of the night.

"Do we?" she asked now.

Jake shrugged. Traffic and paddle shifters on the steering wheel meant that he had to have both hands and much of his mind on the wheel.

"He has always had his own interpretation of honor," Jake offered. "Rules. Maybe to make up for all the laws he was breaking along the way. I agree with your assessment that it might be a trap, but there's risk in everything we do. That's part of what makes Pacific Force work."

"We're willing to go in where others won't?" she asked.

"We'll go in immediately, where some governments will dither too long," he said. "Carefully, where others will overreact and send excessive force. Look at all the people the US Government bombs in Afghanistan or Iraq or wherever else, hitting them with drone-mounted missile strikes and killing everybody at a wedding, just to get one guy. I'm not about to say we should go in places like that, but I'm also uncertain what's gained by making more enemies instead of letting them have their own country. Look how badly the West screwed up Iran, after all."

He felt her nod out of the corner of her eye. Her family had been deposed by the oil companies, way back, because they wouldn't play ball with the Brits or the Americans. Then the guy the West brought in to replace her family had turned out to be a megalomaniac who got himself overthrown, with Hollyanne's parents and relatives forced to flee in the dead of night to Switzerland or other places, before some of them ended up in the US.

"Could Nathaniel call for help?" she asked. "That's almost what this feels like."

"Flip it on its head," Jake replied. "Why would he call us for help? What would prevent him from just stepping around a corner and vanishing? Not like he hasn't done that before."

"Somebody had a gun to his head?" she asked.

"Assumedly," Jake nodded. "But they'd slip up. Everybody has to relax at some point and Nathaniel can be amazingly charming when he wants to be."

"Granted," Hollyanne acknowledged. "He'd hook up with other criminals. It's Nathaniel. Going straight is probably mentally and emotionally impossible these days. What does he find?"

"Something scary enough that he can't find an easy way out," Jake said. "Something big enough to frighten him."

"Something too delicate for a government to handle without collateral damage everywhere," Hollyanne added. "Or leaks. Nathaniel would want out, but not at the cost of him going back to prison. Or getting killed by a missile coming in the window."

"Tightrope walk," Jake nodded. "So he has to call in someone who might make him that deal."

"Would we?" she countered. "Would you make Nathaniel a deal that lets him walk away from something and not go back to prison?"

"Theoretically?" he asked, glancing over until she nodded. "Sure. I have no idea what, but we're not a government. We are a privately-financed mercenary security operation. There are a lot of those out there, but most of them are either defensive in nature, like bodyguards, or thinly-disguised brownshirt fascist organizations that eventually drift over into petty crime and terrorism. Look at a lot of biker gangs, and by that I mean bad men and not dentists having their mid-life crisis. Or take

Charlottesville, Virginia, and that idiot who drove into a crowd of protesters because he honestly didn't seem to think that killing anyone would be a problem."

"It's going to get worse," Hollyanne replied, sounding like an oracle now. "That fool in the White House is playing with fire."

"All the more reason the world needs something like Pacific Force," Jake said. "Global fire brigade that doesn't blow up the village in the process of saving it."

"So I have a theoretical for you then, Jake," she said. "Last time, Nathaniel was expecting us to take our time getting to England. That's why he moved so quickly. We got off our asses and got inside his decision-making curve so we were there when we needed to be. Same here, but I'm not sure the Germans will be as open-minded and forgiving as the Brits."

"With you so far," he replied.

"Too much risk of delaying too long and not being there," she said. "At the same time, we don't want to be in Germany too early, because someone might recognize us and tighten their operational security, thus screwing up Nathaniel's plans."

"Okay."

"So maybe you call Sir William in London, or wherever he is," Hollyanne offered. "Ask if he had anything like those Chechen punks in the UK that we might hit in the next few days. That puts us on Nathaniel's side of the Atlantic, but not so close that people freak. He would likely see that we'd gotten his message, since we can't communicate with him directly. Then we can move on short notice."

"I like it," he replied. "Carrie is fixing dinner and will leave cooking instructions. You can explain it to everyone.

I'll make that call when we get home and see what he knows."

Her sigh sounded heavy, but they all had unfinished business with Nathaniel.

Even if they might end up on the same side for a while.

CHAPTER
NINE

NATHANIEL HAD KEPT his head down. Generally avoided people whenever possible. Safer that way, at least with this group of genocidal yahoos. GC was able to handle most of the day-to-day tech support operations, since it wasn't like you could hire a call center team with handy scripts when you were a criminal organization.

The US and UK governments notwithstanding.

Some of the tasks, however, got escalated. Nathaniel had noted a pattern whereby it seemed to be mostly females that he had to deal with. The really pretty ones, usually. Gothic Chip would make one half-assed attempt to fix whatever, then foist them off on him.

Dead Eve and Lady Nyx were two that ended up in his office. Lady Nyx was generally pleasant to be around. Dead Eve was...*special.*

She made you think of a crazed lunatic, even sitting perfectly still and quiet. Part of it was those beady eyes, the color of blueberries. Nathaniel had never seen blue eyes that dark. Thick, curly, gold hair worn medium-length and in a simple, businesslike style might make you think of a saleswoman.

Until she opened her mouth.

Technophobe. Homicidal nutjob technophobe.

And Gothic Chop had passed the woman one to him to deal with. Possibly because Dead Eve was short, muscular, and athletic. Attractive to look at. Exactly the opposite of GC in many ways, to the point Nathaniel wondered if GC had even more issues underneath everything else that didn't come to the surface often.

And Dead Eve was absolutely *not* someone you wanted to fall asleep next to, for fear of waking up in a bathtub full of ice, missing a kidney.

Plus, she liked knives. Like, in a scary kind of way. Even dressed out of costume, or whatever you called it when someone wore a blue button-up shirt and faded blue jeans instead of gray tactical gear with a red and black costume color theme, she had a knife in her boot, another on her hip, and a third strapped to her right forearm for a crossdraw slash.

Today, her phone was being wonky.

Still, she was being awful flirty for someone needing her phone triaged.

"Can you fix it, Moriarty?" Dead Eve asked in a whiny voice that by itself would probably be enough to not call for a second date. Unless she'd been that good in bed.

Nathaniel wasn't ever going to claim to be a saint.

As with the rest of them, nobody had a simple name. No Daves or Amandas, though that would change if they ever got arrested.

Grown-ups, LARPing through the world, which would be okay if it didn't involve live weapons and occasional dead bodies.

Dead Eve had unlocked the device before handing it to him. His inherited office was still a mess, but getting better as he got things filed, sorted, or burned to get them out of his way. Nathaniel's preference would be for maybe one-tenth as much crap if he had to find any tools.

Right now, he only needed his mind.

First things first, he had rebooted it, wondering when was the last time she'd bounced the thing. That had helped. Now, he was onto the update screen, trying not to scream at the woman.

"You haven't updated any of your apps in two years?" he asked carefully. Delicately.

This was a woman with a penchant for knives.

Black widow in more ways than one.

"Never," she smiled happily. "That way, they can't insert anything to track me."

Nathaniel kept his opinions to himself. She played a half-dozen different brain-candy games on this phone. And carried it with her everywhere. Had nobody ever explained what cell towers were to her? Or did she think it was all just magic?

Nathaniel refused to ask, deeply concerned about the answer he might get.

Idiot savant in some ways. Genius level potential, but incredibly narrow in focus. All of everyone else's average, squished into homicidal lunacy, leaving her hopeless at a lot of other things.

Socialization seemed to be one of things that was missing.

"I'll need to talk to Lord Wraith," Nathaniel said. "Get some clarifications from him before I make any drastic changes. But yes, I should be able to fix it after that."

She bounced up like a kid that had just won a spelling bee but felt at least a decade older than that. Still a decade younger than him.

Shit, when had he turned into the mature adult in the room?

Again, trick question. Everything relative to these people.

Still, she grabbed her phone and vanished.

Nathaniel gave her a two-minute head start, shaking his head for the most part, then followed.

Eventually, he got through the layers of security and paranoia keeping Lord Wraith isolated from the rest of them.

Nathaniel just assumed that the man had been wearing pajamas or something comfortable and needed time to get into costume before meeting one of his minions. Everyone else around here was in a costume of some sort.

Nathaniel had been smart enough to pick one that he could emulate with simple tan slacks and an old blazer in herringbone tweed. No makeup. No fancy armor or exotic weaponry.

An island of sanity, which just made this whole extravaganza all the more frightening.

A goon in a faceless mask escorted him into Lord Wraith's inner sanctum. Nathaniel wondered which old occult detective movie the man had used as a model for the room as he sat across the desk from his nominal boss.

Library, in sense of built-in bookshelves with leather tomes. Odd trophies that probably either had sentimental value or came with the package when you ordered an evil genius's lair from some catalog.

Was there a catalog for this sort of thing? Should he look at starting one? Easy way to make money off people with lots of cash and no aesthetic sense.

Not today's problem. Maybe next week's.

"Yes, Moriarty?" Lord Wraith asked as they got settled on opposites sides of the man's big, oak desk.

Lord Wraith didn't wear a mask inside the base but did when dealing with governments and reporters. Today he was in black robes over black pants, like some weird Supreme Court justice, with six, separate, white hashmarks on each upper arm like rank or something. Better than Dead Eve. Not as fashionable as Lady Nyx.

Just as shithouse rat crazy.

"Dead Eve has a phone that needs some basic maintenance," Nathaniel said simply, like this was an everyday conversation between two guys in an office and not the lair of a world-ending villain leaning onto his next scheme.

"And?"

"And she has never allowed it to be updated with fixes since she bought it," Nathaniel said. "Before I did, I wanted to make sure you didn't forbid that sort of thing for reasons I haven't been told yet. If I am okay to fix it, did you want me to set up a series of multi-continental defensive proxies to shield the data stream, or just go into town and handle it at a coffee shop, like before?"

The man's eyes glazed over a little at the technical jargon, as expected. He'd apparently originally thought that GC was a bad-ass cybersecurity expert when Nathaniel would have put her low on the third tier of a helpdesk. More than adequate to most tasks. Not ready for management in her thinking.

"Which would be easier?" Lord Wraith asked, a little lost.

"Me going outside the walls introduces risk," Nathaniel said. "I'm a wanted man and someone might recognize me. Doing it inside means that there is a risk some government or hacker collective looks at those proxies as a challenge and tried to attack our firewall. Nobody really knows we're here, and I like it that way. If someone started to aim significant resources at us, they might get in and see whatever you have in your files. I'd rather not."

"Absolutely not!" Lord Wraith thundered. "You should go outside to do that."

Nathaniel nodded. Safer for the organization. And what he really wanted anyway.

"I'd like to handle this like an op, then," he said, shifting his tones from co-worker to special agent. "Go out in three days but take Lady Nyx with me instead of Dead Eve. Same coffee shop, like the two of us were on a second date or something, just in case someone is watching that might remember me from before and wonder if I showed up with a new girlfriend. That also isolates us from bringing anyone down on you. Since I've been seen with Lady Nyx previously, bringing Dead Eve might cause someone to remember and question. We don't want to leave a memory there, in case someone sees a wanted poster later."

"Yes," Lord Wraith said, nodding as if all that sounded brilliant, instead of a pile of hokum. "You organize it that way. And come up with a long-term plan to keep all our systems up-to-date. If Dead Eve has done it, likely the others have as well."

"If we had more time, I'd suggest setting up a secondary network," Nathaniel offered. "Air-gap it inward, since many of our systems don't need to be facing the fire-wall. Probably all but two of them. Then come up with programmatic processes to bridge the gap nightly without risking the organization."

"You do not have time?" he asked, still confused and a little bamboozled.

"I've noticed that your operational tempo has started to increase," Nathaniel said carefully, though in a nonchalant manner. And without mentioning what he'd accidentally gotten from GC. "That suggests that the big operation is coming sooner rather than later. If we are somehow bringing down all satellite communications, most of the hackers and players I'm concerned about will cease being a problem because the wires in place now won't be able to handle all that network traffic. And will have to flow through terrestrial nodes where others might take notice and block them off entirely."

"Oh…" Lord Wraith replied in a cross-eyed kind of way. "Still, it won't be sudden. And it won't destroy the world. We will talk again before it happens."

Nathaniel decided that that sounded like a good dismissal and rose.

"Thank you, sir," he nodded, backing away quickly while the getting was good.

Outside, he kept his sigh of exasperation inside. Too many faceless goons in masks around him.

This would all be a joke if it wasn't for two things.

One, they were all killers.

Two, they might succeed.

CHAPTER
TEN

SPENCER WASN'T the brains of the organization. No, that was Jake. But he was the reporter, forever digging. The hacker, with ties and skills down into those dark parts of the internet where most people don't even have the tools to navigate.

He'd seen some shit in his time.

Right now, they were finishing off the meal Carrie had left for them. Chicken in a cream sauce, cooked with simple drop biscuits over top. Comfort food, the kind that the woman always seemed to know would work best.

Wine, beer, and juice were being consumed. Spencer had a decaf mocha from Jake's coffee robot on the counter behind him.

"So right now, England lets us into Germany pretty easily," Spencer explained. "We're all up to date on visas and shots, so nobody will care much. However—and this is a big however, gang—we're still Pacific Force. If we fly commercial, even separately, someone is likely to notice. US and UK governments at a dead minimum, plus whoever wants to hack the various FAA and related data streams. Alternatively, if we fly together, it promises to be a circus when we land. Wherever we land. Do we fly in secretly?"

"I've spoken with Sir William," Jake said quietly. "He's passing on our request to drop in and spend some time local to London or whenever, with a hard stop no later than three days before Nathaniel's date, so we can get into position. I expect to hear back from them tomorrow morning our time with an update."

Spencer nodded. Sir William was a spook. Retired now and acting as something of a liaison between the Palace and whoever was Her Majesty's Government right now. May was PM now and trying to complete some sort of Brexit, after Cameron had fucked everything up. She was attempting to do just about the dumbest thing Spencer could think of, but everybody assumed that they would chicken out or fail eventually. If not, the Russians might start a new Cold War. Maybe win it this time.

"If we fly private, chances are that we can carry arms, but how closely will Britain or Germany watch us?" Rik asked. "Last time, it was my bow, and their laws have a couple of loopholes I don't intend to tell them about."

"Uhm…" Grant spoke up now, hemming and hawing and licking his lips.

Everyone stopped to watch him.

"I went ahead and had a chat with a friend," he continued. "A guy, you see, who knows a guy. You know how it goes."

"Belize, again?" Hollyanne asked, smiling but serious.

"No, but a friend of his," Grant nodded with a quick grin. "A cousin, if you believe him, but they all have cousins. Anyway. Favors exchanged and a little cash could get us access to an armorer who knows her stuff. Mostly works in movies, so she has a stupid collection of guns in all sizes and shapes, plus permits to own and modify them as needed."

"We filing off serial numbers here?" Jake asked.

"No, because they might come filed off," Grant squinted and turned his head a little sideways. "Or maybe from the factory without any in the first place, because they were never intended to be sold on the open market. Movies, you know."

"We likely to burn her?" Spencer asked.

"Doubtful," Grant nodded. "Solid rep in the right places. Money under the table. If we threw in a little signed merch, that would go a long way on expenses."

Spencer laughed with the rest of them. At the end of the day, they were still Pacific Force, with their own comic book, about half true and half fanciful bullshit. At least until somebody writing it got bored or ran out of material and decided to bring in aliens, paranormal, or do a steampunk western reboot.

All Jake had to do, though, was fill in some of the stories that Verónica hadn't been privy to yet, and she would probably be good for another five years, during which Pacific Force would be saving the world.

Again.

Jake turned to Rik.

"Got any Issue One reprints handy?" he asked her. "Or a poster we can all sign and personalize thanking her for things she won't be at liberty to discuss?"

"Lemme check the trunk," Rik replied with a grin.

Originally, the comic book had been her idea. And Verónica was somebody she knew from way back. Maybe an ex-girlfriend, though Spencer had never asked. She wrote and drew the issues, with a rotating cast for folks doing inking and color.

They sold pretty damned well, from the checks that came in regularly.

"Okay, then," Jake said turning back. "If they want us doing something in England, they can supply Rik the weapons when we get there. Grant, you work with Germany and Rik to coordinate that end. As for transit, I propose that we head out tomorrow afternoon and red-eye. I've reached out to that same friend that let us borrow his jet last time. He's in Ensenada right now and doesn't need it, so we can fly discreetly. Just like before. No weapons but bring whatever gear you think you'll need for London, then get Grant your wishlist for Germany. Questions?"

Spencer had a bunch, but he and Jake would go over that later. Tactical minutiae, rather than big stuff. Who was talking in the shadows. What they were saying. Stuff like that.

To Spencer, it was like breathing, so he acted as something of a filter for the rest of the team.

And nobody out there was talking about anything big enough to frighten Nathaniel.

How bad was it going to get?

CHAPTER
ELEVEN

JAKE HAD SPOKEN with Sir William briefly before the flight, but once the man knew that they were headed to England, Sir William had simply made arrangements for Jake to meet with him in his City of London office, not all that far from Downing Street.

One of the quieter places, if there was such a thing. Not inside the innermost ring of security, but only one step outward from the center.

Two cars had met them at the small, private airport where the plane was being stored. One for the team to get to the hotel, the other for Jake to go directly into London.

The man driving had become generally known these days as *Steve*. It wasn't his real name, but that had been the name he had given Grant last spring, when they'd first returned to hunt Nathaniel. It was good enough for today as well.

Steve hadn't spoken at all beyond the basics for the hour drive to Sir William's office.

"We're here," Steven announced unnecessarily as they pulled into an underground lot and parked.

Jake nodded and followed the man into the elevator and up to the top of the building.

Sir William, when they got into his office, was dressed in his usual manner, a high-level bureaucrat in severe gray with razored pinstripes. Dark hair brushed back and gray above the ears. Lean muscles in a manner similar to Jake's. Wise, hazel eyes.

Originally, the future Sir William had managed to get himself into Eton on a scholarship, then on to Cambridge, both times because he boxed. After that, down into the rabbit hole of British Intelligence, emerging thirty-some years later with a KBE for activities not discussed in polite company.

Jake sat in one chair on this side of the desk. Steve was in the other, which had surprised Jake, but only for a moment. Probably setting the man up as a minder for the team while in England.

Once they got tea and small talk out of the way, Sir William turned deadly serious.

"What's going on in Germany?" he asked bluntly.

Jake did appreciate that about the man. Other bureaucrats, the kind who had gone into politics after Cambridge, would have hemmed and hawed around any number of topics for an hour before asking, saying almost nothing.

"A criminal," Jake volleyed, just as bluntly. "We have a lead on a location and date because someone is setting him up. Pacific Force intends to be there to capture said suspect."

"Is it Hoestler?" Sir William asked.

It had only been a few months since British operatives had allowed Nathaniel to slip through their fingers again, after Jake and the team had managed to thwart his operation and capture all of his people.

"I'm not at liberty to discuss," Jake answered, not

smiling. "And, as it happens to be in Germany, you have no jurisdiction until such time as we turn our quarry over to local law enforcement. Then you can ask your counterparts in the BRD for a favor. They might grant it."

"Would you allow one of our agents to accompany you?" Sir William pressed, nodding to Steve.

"Why?" Jake countered bluntly.

Since Sir William had been blunt with him, Jake had no problems being blunt in return. He could do that with Sir William. One of the few people on this island who wouldn't immediately draw offense and get all pissy.

"He broke out of an English prison," Sir William said. "That makes him a fugitive from our justice, even if Germany and other places might wish to put in for extradition on their own merits."

"Your folks have lost him six times, Sir William," Jake reminded the man, perhaps playing a little rough. "Twice in a row now he's actually been under arrest and gotten away, with one of those from the highest security prison you have. The American Supermax in Colorado might be able to hold him. I'm not sure how many other joints could."

"And you will not bend?" Sir William asked.

"I appreciate the offer of assistance," Jake offered as a mollification. "But this operation will be tight and risky. I can't bring in a stranger at the last minute, however well trained and capable, and not add what I believe is one too many vectors of instability. That being said, if Steve here were in western Germany in a week, perhaps on vacation or maybe consulting with some allies on the continent, he might be close enough to respond to a call, once the operation was complete and our fugitive in hand."

"You haven't answered my original question, Jake," he said. "Is it Hoestler?"

"And I won't answer it, Sir William," Jake nodded. "Not until we're done and I have someone apprehended. I don't trust anybody outside this office to keep their mouth shut. Too much money and blackmail material floating around. Someone would tell someone else a secret, *ad nauseam*, and pretty soon the whole world will be standing around pretending to be tourists with telephoto lenses and tripping over each other. And it will only get worse over time."

"What do you mean?"

"Brexit," Jake said. "You're leaving the EU. Not the biggest surprise, considering how little the UK has liked being a member. But what happens when you are no longer part of one of the biggest trading blocs in the world? When your economy has to compete with the rest of the folks outside because you won't have access to the continent's markets on fair terms?"

"The government would never let it come to that," Sir William countered, but Jake wasn't convinced. He could see the first stirrings of fear in the man's eyes.

"Have any of the folks at the top given you any reason to believe that they could find their own asses with both hands, a map, and a flashlight, Sir William?" Jake asked.

Steve gasped. Sir William gaped. Jake remained serious.

"My single greatest fear right now, beyond Brexit, is the Union itself," Jake said. "What happens if trade between Ireland and the North has to go back to the hard walls? Do the Troubles start up again after everything everybody did in the 90s to bring peace? Or Scotland? How soon until folks up north rile up enough voters to demand their own exit from the Union? What happens if the Act of Union is undone? If you thought Russian criminal money was bad in London now, imagine how bad it could get in another decade, Sir William."

"What would you suggest?" the man asked carefully.

"Not my problem to solve," Jake replied, softening the hardness of his face with a quick shrug. "England wanted out and is getting it. I still think the general population has been sold a pig in a poke. On the one hand, international crime probably gets worse over the next several years because the UK and the US both seem to be intent on imploding. Again, I suspect Russian and Chinese money behind it, though mostly Russian because the Chinese just want to tweak our President, not destroy their single biggest trading partner. Taiwan isn't worth their own economy imploding. You'd be back to the Thirties and Forties quickly at that point. With a lot of angry neighbors who wanted to pay China back for all the meddling of centuries. Pacific Force will continue doing what we do, at least as long as folks want us around and continue to offer rewards commensurate with risk."

"There is an amazing bounty on Hoestler's head," Sir William perked up. "Not just British money, either. Many people want a piece of him."

"We will burn that bridge when we get there," Jake nodded. "Was there something beyond that we could chat about? Pacific Force is available for about a week before we have to travel on. Normally, we'd just be on something of a vacation here, but we're here."

Jake paused and turned to include Steve in the question.

"How can we help you?"

"We have a secondary concern because of your mention of Germany," Sir William said, waiting for Jake to nod. "Have you heard of a new underground movement calling itself *Dark Citizen*?"

CHAPTER
TWELVE

GRANT ASSUMED that somebody was being cute by trying to include Steve in this operation, but he wasn't about to play, even if they could have convinced Jake. On some idiot bureaucrat's ledger, it probably even made sense, as so many people had gotten themselves on Jake's shit list last time around. They would want someone who had been seen as helpful. Especially after Jake had burned a few folks when they'd pushed him far enough last time.

Today, Grant wanted no help. No outsiders. Nobody messing with things, because most of the people he would want to talk to in London could spot a Peeler a mile away.

And, unfortunately, Steve smelled like a cop, which was why he didn't get to go anywhere with Grant, most of the time. Including today.

Not enough time deep cover, Grant assumed. Badge and gun kind of agent, who kicked in doors and arrested everyone in the joint, rather than a tapeworm that quietly infiltrated someplace and bled it dry from the inside.

Not that Grant ever stayed around any of his cons and infiltrations long enough. Like marriage, that way, and Grant had tried that enough times. Divorced from two of them, as far as he knew, though jurisdictions and legal issues might mean he had more than one wife he didn't remember.

Common law could get weird in some places. London was like that.

Today, he was north of the river and south of Buckingham. One of those amazingly touristy zones where real estate was stupidly expensive and lots of folks with Russian accents, or at least mail order brides, running around. Plus Middle Eastern oil princes and extended families.

Money.

Grant wasn't in their league, but he also wasn't here to grift them out of a chunk.

Today. You never knew with some of these silly punks.

Today, he was playing tourist. The others were back at the hotel doing their thing. Jake had given him a name and a check-in time. Dangerous combination, because that meant Grant was operating without adult supervision.

He smiled at the thought. London was probably doomed as a result.

He smelled the joint while still a block away. Near Sloane Square, where some of the cars parked on the street cost more than a lot of software nerds in Seattle back home made in a year.

Oil. Hot, greasy fish fried in it, along with chips. Malt vinegar that was somehow embedded in the sidewalk itself like a culinary aphrodisiac.

Grant wondered if someone just painted light poles with the stuff in a radius to draw them in. He should prob-ably ask Murad. Then suggest it. It had his stomach rumbling even before he slipped in the door.

Not quite bedlam, but it was early in the day for the tourists used to New York time. Still crowded. One of the most classically *English'Fish'N'Chips* places you could get in London. The spot where tourists came for the authentic experience, rubbing elbows with the billionaires and aristocrats for grub.

Murad was standing behind the main counter, watching the place like a hungry hawk. He spotted Grant immediately and nodded him closer. A second nod towards the food, asking if he was hungry.

Uhm, duh?

They both smiled and Murad tapped a waitress going by.

Grant ended up following him down a side corridor towards the loo, then through a locked door and down into the basement. Nothing had changed down here.

Storage room, or something like that. Lots of kegs down here along two walls, along with a space in the corner that had been set up as an office for Murad to do paperwork. Murad sat behind the desk and gestured to a chair.

As Grant sat, the man pulled two glasses down from a shelf and uncovered that small tap hidden in the wall behind him. He filled both glasses with that nut brown ale that Murad liked and handed one to Grant.

"Surprised to see you again so soon," Murad said. "And you didn't call first. Never good news."

"Like last time, moving fast to get ahead of people," Grant said, aware that every word he told this man would become coin to be traded on later.

Greasing the wheels of underworld commerce. And yet another reason Steve wasn't allowed to hang around when Grant was working. The government took a dim eye towards crime, especially when they couldn't stop it from happening.

"Trouble?" Murad asked, perking up as he sipped.

From above, the sound of the door opening, followed by Murad's grand-niece Senzala bringing a big plate of food down. She smiled this time but didn't speak. Withdrew immediately.

"How soon until you retire?" Grant asked abruptly when they were alone.

Murad was a fixture these days, a Pakistani who even the English Defense League punks left alone. At least those who didn't have a death wish. He'd been here for at least four decades now.

"Soon," Murad nodded. "And yes, Senzala will inherit that side of the business, so next time you come I will formally introduce you. Her mother will run the restaurant itself. She's good at that. Senzala will handle the rest."

"Good," Grant replied, unable to fathom London without Murad in the shadows. "As to trouble, we're not sure. Jake has us here for only a few days before we move on to someplace else. The Palace asked Jake if he could dig up anything on a thing called the Dark Citizen Movement. I figured I'd start at the top and work my way down the scale."

Murad's eyes got pensive, staring over Grant's shoulder at something miles away.

"Normally, I'd say nothing important," Murad replied slowly. "Another one of those back-to-nature cults that society throws up occasionally. Like Utopians or Luddites that way. Or your American Hippies in the old days. The Palace asked Jake to look into it?"

"Tax-paying citizens," Grant nodded. "Upright and square in all the correct ways. Not a threat, but something has them riled up."

"You mentioned a next step after this," Murad spoke deliberately. "Germany?"

Grant nodded.

"Dark Citizen seems to have originated there," Murad continued. "Maybe grandchildren of the anti-nuke pacifist movements that gave Reagan such fits."

"What do they actually want?" Grant pressed.

"Something similar to the Luddites," Murad nodded. "Early labor movement concerned that the factory owners were lying, chiseling thieves, cheating workers out of a fair living. Again, these things are circular. Right now, Global Labor is at a low point, so some of the organizations are getting a little militant. Dark Citizen isn't one of them, near as I can tell. They strike me as more likely to turn their backs on the modern world so they might try to carve out a slower place to live."

"Germany, huh?" Grant asked.

"Indeed," Murad agreed. "The British Labour Party is in something of a disarray, because they've manage to elect an unreformed communist who seems to be still getting even with Heath and Thatcher, and maybe even Wilson and Callaghan. And utterly unwilling to maneuver his silly high-horse to carve away soft spots in the Tory flank. Blair was a son of a bitch, but one hell of an operator. Jeremy is a fool."

"So the Germans wouldn't try to maneuver around him?" Grant asked.

"Can't, really," Murad laughed. "He got the rules changed so that the leader of the Party in the Commons is elected in a national plebiscite, and the hard-core locals support him. At least until he blows it on something big and they pick his corpse clean."

"Okay, so Germany might think that Britain is a lost cause," Grant nodded. "Doubly so with Brexit threatening everything. How much Russian money is behind them? We just had to take down a rogue group in Los Angeles a few weeks ago. All Chechens who deny anything official, but the weapons were bleeding edge tech, being sold for stupidly low prices."

"Los Angeles was you?" Murad asked, surprised.

Grant grinned.

"Jake wanted it low profile," he nodded. "Brought in Perkins from the Seattle office at the last minute, just to keep the radar clear until we struck."

"Interesting," Murad mused, leaning back and sipping beer.

Grant grabbed a piece of fish that was finally cool and dunked it with that malt vinegar that had been calling him like a siren.

"There is a lot of Russian money floating around," Murad finally continued. "Flooding into the UK and the US equally. I assume that midget KGB punk is trying to destabilize things?"

"Sun Tzu covered this," Grant nodded. "Among others. Way cheaper to pay your enemies to destroy themselves than to do it yourself."

"That he did," Murad laughed. "Given that logic, I see no reason to assume that Dark Citizen is on the up and up. Most likely started out as a legitimate social movement, like so many guess. Maybe someone came along later with a briefcase of cash and asked a favor?"

"That's what usually happens," Grant agreed. "Jake hopes that you and your contacts can find some useful intel for the Palace. They won't know where it came from, but they might. If nothing else, certain players will be grateful, or at least less assholish later."

"Less, maybe," Murad laughed with his head back. "Fools in charge. Fools arguing with them across the Chamber. The UK might be right proper fucked this time."

"Would you go back to Pakistan?" Grant asked, intrigued.

"Long Island, more likely," Murad sobered. "Kin there that I could draw on if I needed to relocate the entire clan. Hopefully, your fool in charge is only there for four years and an adult can start cleaning it up afterwards."

"You and me both, Murad," Grant agreed. "Past that, are there any dangerous anarchists around here we might need to say hello to in the next couple of days?"

NATHANIEL LOOKED up as the door opened and Lady Nyx slipped in, dressed again like Amanda, rather than the skin-tight, black-leather-everything outfit that made tongues hang out. Including his when she wasn't looking.

Nathaniel smiled as she took a chair across the desk from him.

The place was still a mess, but that was him no longer really caring if it got cleaned. Plus, he'd been focused… *elsewhere*. Nathaniel had approached this operation like a man going after the Queen's Crown Jewels. Every detail worked out to the meter and the second. Sight lines. Bus patterns. Weather forecasts. Anything that might be important once he walked out the front door, because Nathaniel had no intention of coming back voluntarily.

And now that he had Lady Nyx as a babysitter, the risks were extremely high. On the one hand, Dead Eve wasn't nearly as smart or devious. Honestly, she was almost a one-trick pony. The problem was that that trick was homicide with blades.

Not his preferred outcome.

On the flip-side, there was at least a sliver of a chance that Lady Nyx wanted out as well. Giving him her phone number suggested a time after all this stupidity when he might be running his own shop. At a time when Lord Wraith was intending to disrupt most of the world for a few decades. Most cellular networks relied on satellites, so if those went down, how could he call her?

Or had she maybe been looking for a date? And with him or Jake?

Hard to tell. Impossible to ask, without giving away too much information in the process.

Risk risk risk.

At first, the forecast for drizzle this afternoon had filled him with dismay. The plan called for a stop at an ice cream parlor for a cone. One of those off-kilter moments that looked utterly innocent on the surface of things, while giving Nathaniel a drop zone that wasn't the coffee shop where Lord Wraith might have allies already inserted and watching.

But drizzle suggested a haze that might be useful. Less distance he could be seen. The problem was that Nathaniel was pretty sure Lady Nyx could still drill him dead center at two hundred yards if she really wanted to.

Did she?

"There's news," she said as she settled, still smiling at him but her eyes were darker with concern.

"Oh?" Nathaniel asked, evoking every bit of innocence that he could manage.

"Pacific Force is apparently in England," she told him.

Again, her emotions were hard to read. Rage? Lust? Fear? Something was there, but Nathaniel couldn't find any handle to separate it out into something he could translate.

Of course, he would be the first person to tell you he

didn't understand women. Doubly so when you had a highly intelligent, highly educated killer who looked stunning in just about anything she was wearing. Including today's jeans, sweater, and rain shell.

"England?" Nathaniel confirmed.

Not where he'd expected them, but Jake and the gang had made a career out of surprising Nathaniel in order to upset his plans.

At least this time it might be working in his favor. Hopefully, Spencer had understood the message, and this was all an elaborate misdirection.

"That's right," Lady Nyx nodded. "Spotted a couple of days ago in London by someone we have inside British Intelligence."

Which was exactly why Nathaniel didn't trust anybody but Pacific Force to rescue him. Anything he'd have told any organization out there would have been a single phone call away from reaching Lord Wraith.

"Do we know why?" Nathaniel asked carefully.

Oh, so carefully.

"Jake McNeil met with some bigshots, from what I'm told," she shrugged. "Then Grant Collingwood and Spencer Sargossian started rattling the underworld, supposedly looking for Russian criminal gangs and anarchists."

Nathaniel felt a chill bite, like Death running her fingers across the back of his neck.

Anarchist was just about as perfect a description as you could get to Lord Wraith. And the Dark Citizens he commanded.

That was where Nathaniel parted company with them. He liked civilization. Wanted to partake of the finer things in life, like roads and indoor plumbing.

These lunatics wanted to watch the world burn. Light

the match, even. It was already well on its way to doing that without additional help.

Nathaniel had read scientific studies suggesting that the world had at most twenty years to reverse course before a lot of things global warming started turned utterly destructive. Already, hurricanes hitting Florida with ten times the power that they'd had forty years ago. How soon until droughts and warming caused all of Siberia or Nebraska to catch fire?

"Does Lord Wraith want us to scrub the mission?" Nathaniel asked.

That was really all he cared about. Once he got out of the building and they walked to where a bus would carry them downtown, he was running.

If Pacific Force had come this far, they were probably just around the next corner. At least he hoped so.

Nathaniel had other contacts he could reach out to. Favors he might call in.

Hopefully, someone out there liked him more than they feared Lord Wraith's wrath.

"No," Lady Nyx smiled, still serious though. "He's ordered English operatives into hiding for now. French and German cells are apparently operating at a higher level of security than normal, but they were already ramping up anyway."

Nathaniel nodded. Sometime in roughly a week, somebody was going to launch a rocket. That rocket had racks of smaller satellites inside, both cubesats and larger-though-still-small units like the new internet communications satellites that the South African guy wanted to fill the night with, thereby winning the billionaire space race.

Which was what caused one of the other billionaires, who saw himself losing, to step up and sabotage the entire thing.

Nathaniel had been unable to penetrate the right files to know more than that. Even looking would have marked him as a spy to be questioned sharply and maybe executed. It had been enough that he'd gotten a message out, supposedly to his brokers, who had quietly liquidated his various holdings.

Those messages had been real. It had only been Cleveland—the message to Spencer—that had been a red herring. If Lord Wraith still succeeded in spite of Jake, Nathaniel wanted to not be broke.

Whatever else happened.

He studied Lady Nyx closely. Bright blue eyes he really hadn't processed before. Almost steel blue, compared to the blueberry craziness of Dead Eve.

"Are you comfortable with this operation?" he asked.

"Sure," she nodded. "Though I think that you've gone a little overboard for what really only amounts to a coffee date."

Coffee date? Really?

"In this game, there are necessary actions, and mistakes," he replied, quoting some old book on strategy and tactics he had absorbed somewhere along the line. "Given the timing and the fact that Pacific Force is much closer that we'd been expecting, I want to make sure that this is not a mistake. Mistakes are what have caused me the most problems over the years. Trusting the wrong people, usually."

"Am I a wrong person?" Lady Nyx suddenly leaned forward and glaring at him. Just a bit.

"You planning to double-cross me at some point?" he fired back, staying in character as the deadly *Moriarty*, the cybersecurity mastermind of the modern age.

"Not planning to," she countered. "You?"

Nathaniel considered his words carefully before he spoke.

"You would be the last person around here I would betray," he replied. "All the rest first, because while there are smart ones and deadly ones out there, you're the one around here who combines the two into the most formidable package."

Her eyes blinked a couple of times. Might not be used to compliments in her own language.

Not his problem.

Hell of a woman.

If only he'd met her *anywhere* else.

"So," Nathaniel said after that pause for her to get her brain on track. "Interest you in a coffee date?"

"I thought you'd never ask."

JAKE PREFERRED DOING things with subtlety and guile. Sneak up on the bad guys and ambush them from an unexpected angle.

Full frontal assaults were for Marines who thought that was a smart way to solve a problem.

Being noisy in London and Manchester rubbed him the wrong way, even though he stopped to remind himself that he was being sneaky this way.

The English underground had certainly spooked, like a colony of meercats spotting hawks or eagles flying close by. Everyone had gone to ground and pulled in the hole with them.

He was in a pub near Camden today, just him and Grant. The others were off doing other things. Mostly being seen sniffing at various doors to see who panicked.

"What do we know?" Jake asked.

Grant sipped at some nut-brown beer and grinned.

"I suspect that criminal misconduct and losses to crime will be down at least ten percent this quarter," Grant replied. "At least in retrospect a year from now."

Jake nodded. About what he expected. There were teams and squads out there that would wisely bail on whatever operation they had planned, be it armored car job, kidnapping, or even just online hooliganism.

One of the advantages of Pacific Force being in the neighborhood. Too bad nobody would be scared straight as a result.

Jake always felt like that ancient English king who had ordered the tides to stop and drowned when they didn't listen.

Hopefully, he would know when it was time to walk away. Or should he start looking to organize some of their fan clubs into strike teams? Start recruiting a next generation of Pacific Force who could start to take over when he and everybody hit forty? It was a young person's game.

"You just went deadly serious quiet," Grant noted, glancing back over a shoulder for a ghost nobody but Jake could see.

"Had a thought," Jake muttered quietly, sipping his own beer and considering his words carefully. "We're all mid-thirties now. Peak physical condition and all that. How long can we keep doing this?"

"As long as crime and dumbshits continue," Grant answered evenly. "We've never been door-kickers. Hollyanne and Rik are both in better shape now than they were at twenty. More training. Hell, even I jog these days. We've got a decade, I think."

"Then what?" Jake asked. "Let the world go to hell? Or drown in the rising tide?"

"Okay, I stand corrected," Grant grimaced. "You've gone morbid. What's up?"

"Getting old," Jake nodded. "Been fighting Nathaniel for a decade or more. Plus all those other fools out there. More today than there used to be. Why is that?"

It was Grant's turn to get serious as Jake drank some beer.

"In the movies, they say your heroes are only as good, only as memorable, as your villains," Grant said. "Books, too. We've always had Nathaniel. When we took him down, we retired, thinking that we'd finally won. Except that we hadn't. Not with him. Not with others. And yeah, I see more people getting into the act, at least on the bad side of things. Popular culture, maybe?"

"The movies are filled with demigods in spandex saving the world these days," Jake nodded. "But that's a reaction to underlying things. People want that in their lives because they don't see it every day. Or hardly at all. Back a century ago when cops were seen as bad, private detectives stepped in to dispense justice in books and movies. Then secret agents. Military special forces agents more recently. And now heroes who can fly. And still, people are iffy about cops and governments fixing their problems."

"Look around," Grant laughed. "Can you fault them?"

"How so?"

"Corruption, especially here and back home," Grant noted. "Old standards of behavior breaking down. Partly, they never really worked, but partly you have people who flat refuse to be bound by the courtesies of decent behavior these days. Pacific Force is extra-governmental. We can go where they can't. Will go. But can we save the world? I doubt it. As you said, rising tide."

"I was wondering if we needed to do some formal recruiting," Jake offered now, feeling his way along in the dark. "We're a decade into this, plus a little. Maybe we need to find more folks to help. And I don't mean out fan clubs or food kitchens, though those are useful, too. People who will stand up. I'd say get involved with politics, but that immediately cuts things into three pieces, when unity is the outcome we need."

"Right, left, lazy," Grant nodded. "I suppose that we would need to identify the forces breaking the world down, and then how to address them. Stop them. Rebuild before the collapse."

Jake leaned in close and dropped his voice low.

"The Russians seem to be of the opinion that if they can't rule the world, nobody else will," Jake murmured. "Why else start flooding the world with guns and money?"

"The only way to really stop bad guys with that much money requires good guys doing the same," Grant murmured back. "Who are the good guys?"

"I remember when one party back home thought the Russians were pure evil," Jake whispered. "Now, they seem beholden to them, but I'm not sure if they can be saved. Too much Kool-aid."

"One man who has tapped into all the racism, neurotic insecurity, and fascist tendencies, and built a movement on them," Grant nodded.

"He only inherited it," Jake said. "I read somewhere recently that said he was really Reagan's tenth term in office, so we're looking at nearly forty years of effort by somebody to turn the world back into the aristocratic hierarchies that the rise of modernism dismantled. Remember, only a century ago you had assholes and emperors exercising supreme and unfettered executive authority via divine right of kings. If the laws are breaking down, that's what's coming back."

"Fascism breeds on animus, whoever your outsider is that must be targeted," Grant agreed. "Racists back home, and here, too. EDL punks, if nobody else. Again, what can we do, save push back?"

"We can be more organized in our pushing," Jake

decided. "We can start talking internally about what kinds of skill sets we would recruit. What sorts of activities we would ask our allies to engage in. What we can do to break the power and control that techbros have amassed over the last generation."

"Bill Gates is doing good things with his money," Grant offered.

"Only because Melinda apparently leaned pretty hard on him to do it," Jake countered. "At least that's the story I've heard, without asking. The ones after him seem more interested in personal power. Or showing off. How many are currently funding research into rocketry? Granted, all that money pushes the state of the art in advanced science, but even a fraction of it might ameliorate hunger and homelessness. If any of them cared. They don't care."

"I take it you don't want to live on Mars?" Grant grinned.

"What kind of employment contract do you suppose you might have to sign to be able to go?" Jake countered with a hard glare. "And could you quit once you got there? Or are you signing up to become a modern peasant to a tech-lord?"

"Yup, you're grumpy," Grant nodded, leaning back now and grinning. "We're saving the world as much as we can. Will it be enough? I got no clue. Can we do more? Let's ask the others and start drawing up plans. But we do have a mission here."

"We do," Jake agreed. "That's what frightens me."

"How so?"

"Nathaniel might find himself in over his head and doesn't trust anybody but us to get him out. Taking into account all we've just talked about, how bad must that be?"

"Shit, I hate it when you're right like that," Grant said.

"Do we need armed support on this one? Heavy Response Teams like law enforcement agencies routinely use?"

"No," Jake said. "But what about next time?"

CHAPTER
FIFTEEN

RIK HAD OVERWATCH TODAY. She didn't have a sniper rifle. She also hoped that she wouldn't need it.

She stood out around here. Tall and blonde as a Dutch tourist. Curvy in ways that would get people looking at her.

Which was exactly wrong for this mission. Bonn needed quiet. For now.

So she was driving instead. A mostly blacked out, four-door Suburban that Grant had borrowed from some friends. Someone had rebuilt the engine. Not a great job, but better than factory. Gas mileage was shit, but it had a lot of horsepower and class one armor on the doors to stop pistols.

Rik never asked who Grant's friends were.

The 2017 model that Jake had parked back home was a better vehicle, but this one would do. Hopefully, nobody needed guns.

She was parked down the block and across, in such a way that she was looking directly at an ice cream shop that was supposedly today's mission. Coffee from the small shop across the street and down some had let her settle in and watch.

Tourist traffic. Mid-day after lunch. People walking around, doing all the touristy things, plus locals hitting shops for whatever. Bonn had been a sleepy university town before it had been turned into the capital of West Germany, and it had happily gone back to being as sleepy as possible when everything moved east.

Pretty old buildings. Lots of trees. Glorious, drizzly weather. Coffee.

"Everybody, I have a couple approaching from the north," Rik said as she picked them up.

Nathaniel was dressed casually. Jeans and a jacket. Holding hands with a tall brunette like they were on a lunch date. The woman was dressed similarly.

"Spencer, are we expecting two?" Rik asked. "Our target has a date with him."

"Negative," Spencer replied over the comm. "Time, date, location, and target, but no mention of two of them."

"Minder?" Grant asked now.

All of them were scattered around the area, in disguise or just out of sight, like Rik.

"Extremely casual, if she's supposed to be a bodyguard or minder," Rik said. "Holding hands and maybe laughing as they walk."

"Are you sure that you've got the right guy?" Jake asked, half kidding and half concerned from his tone.

"Yup," Rik laughed back.

Nathaniel had never figured out girls when they'd been teenagers. Too busy with his grandiose plans for taking over the world. And Rik couldn't remember reading any intelligence suggesting that he'd ever found a serious rela-tionship with a woman as an adult.

"Okay, I have eyes on," Spencer said. "That's definitely our boy. And yes, he brought a date. Do we assume friendly or hostile?"

"Hostile for now," Hollyanne broke in. "We can apologize later if we have to. Anybody trailing our date?"

"Negative here," Rik said. "Pedestrian traffic flow generally running the other way and I don't see anyone trying to keep up with them."

"Other watchers in place?" Jake asked.

"Doing a good job if there are," Grant chimed in. "I've been shopping for new shirts and picked up some cookies for everyone for later. Nothing has stood out from the background pattern."

Pattern.

Rik understood it, though she wasn't nearly the expert that the others were. At least until it came to guns and cars. Then she could listen to the engine idling at a stoplight and diagnose the problem. Spencer did it with data.

Grant and Jake could do it with people.

Ergo, no watchers had been obvious. That was likely to change shortly, however.

Nathaniel was moving into the target zone.

And he'd brought himself a date.

CHAPTER
SIXTEEN

NATHANIEL HELD Amanda's hand and pretended to be Dave. One of those weird scenarios where maybe he hadn't walked out on the future Pacific Force. Or maybe had managed to sell his game for cash before the collapse that ruined so many technology start-ups in 2000.

Might-have-beens.

Could he have just been walking down a street in Germany on the way to get ice cream and maybe coffee with a beautiful woman who understood some of his more obscure literary jokes?

Frightening.

Because she had a rain shell on, there was space for Lady Nyx to have one of her Berettas, possibly under an arm. So he'd paid attention to her chest. More attention than normal. Bumped into her as they walked, just so his arm might feel the rigid, steel edge of a pistol or the strap of a holster.

Nothing.

He presumed instead that she'd tucked it into the over-sized purse over her other shoulder. It looked heavy, but he had no idea what a woman might carry in a small knapsack.

Guys did pockets. At least cargo pants were largely out of fashion these days, except with certain fascist social movements for which they were practically a uniform.

Nathaniel had Dead Eve's phone tucked into his back pocket, along with a wallet he'd been given after he arrived.

Lord Wraith had taken everything else Nathaniel had brought with him and likely disposed of it to destroy bugs and trackers. Good paranoia, and it wasn't like Nathaniel had accumulated anything he would miss, save for a Brighton & Hove Albion F.C. tie he had liked.

Those were available online, once he got out of here and settled someplace safe.

Or at least safer. Probably nowhere on Earth was safe for him right now.

And here he was, leaping out of the frying pan and hoping somebody caught him before it was the fire.

Right on cue, Nathaniel stopped walking and looked around.

As expected, Lady Nyx reappeared in the space where Amanda had been standing an eyeblink earlier.

"Problem?" she asked, head already on a swivel.

"Something you said earlier," Nathaniel said, pulling on her hand and drawing her more around to face him.

Not square, but paying attention. Looking over his shoulder tactically at glass storefronts, from the way her eyes danced back and forth.

"Oh?" she asked, still deadly incarnate, for all she looked relaxed to anyone more than five feet away.

"Coffee date," Nathaniel offered. "Something a little less formal than an operation that gets me out of the lair and into the sunlight. Or drizzle in this case."

Her eyes stopped racing around and settled on his.

"Okay?" she asked, almost transforming back to Amanda. At least a little.

"Is it okay to call this a coffee date?" Nathaniel asked, heart hammering with nerves.

And not just because she might shoot him.

"You're serious?" she asked, eyes getting a little bigger.

"I could be," he countered. "But that's kind of up to you. Say the word and we'll go back to a mission."

She studied his face. His eyes. Staring deep.

Then she relaxed, and Nathaniel felt his heart start to slow down.

Lady Nyx even smiled.

"I'd like that," she said slowly. Her accent became more pronounced when she got nervous. North London or Camden, before it verged over into something more Midlands.

And she was suddenly far less self-assured.

Like maybe she'd been in the same situation as him. Too nerdy in her own way to know how to handle an emotional thing.

Nathaniel smiled and wondered about those might-have-beens.

He looked around and just happened to note that they had stopped not quite in front of an ice cream shop he'd seen on the previous jaunt.

Tiny place. Counter down the left and wrapped around, with ice cream in glass freezers for you to look at as you picked something, plus various chocolates and treats you could buy. Four small tables for two along the right, all currently occupied. Not as many ice cream flavors as the big American chain, but respectable.

He had looked them up online and counted his options.

"How do you feel about getting some ice cream?" he asked, marveling that his voice didn't break once as he spoke. Didn't catch. Didn't anything.

"Ice cream?" she asked, a little mystified. "Isn't it a little too cold?"

"Not for me," he said. "And it's not like I'm in a hurry to get back and crawl into my lair and hide from the sun or anything. I've got a date with beautiful woman to enjoy. And no idea when she might say yes again."

Her smile might have lit up a dark room.

"Yes," she said, still grinning.

Nathaniel nodded and turned to the shop, still holding her right hand so she couldn't suddenly reach into her purse and pull out a gun. Not that it mattered much, because she was ambidextrous when it came to killing, but it might stop her first flinch.

He took a step and drew her forward, holding the door and following her in.

Lots of flavors. Lots of options. A few customers in line and others enjoying their cups and cones.

He watched Lady Nyx move off to one side, bending over to study flavors as he watched her bottom.

A chance glance to the right and he caught the eyes of a woman in a full Niqab, a blue, hooded garment that some Muslim women wore in public. Not as bad as a Burka, because it left the eyes and nose uncovered.

Scated at the end facing front. She was staring right at him and Nathaniel felt a spike of embarrassment run through, that he'd been caught staring at Lady Nyx's bottom.

Then the woman grinned behind her cloth, a movement that came all the way up to her eyes.

Nathaniel had to control his breathing to not gasp aloud or jump.

That was Hollyanne Kadjar.
Pacific Force was here.

HOLLYANNE HAD BEEN LISTENING to the others chatter about Nathaniel and his supposed body-guard, but when the two entered the shop, it was obvious the woman was far more than that.

The man hadn't mentioned a girlfriend in his message, but she supposed that it might not be a code that he could have sent to Spencer in an email that someone else might read.

Hollyanne had gotten here early and enjoyed a cup of chocolate fudge ice cream, pulling the bottom part of her Niqab down to eat.

Because they hadn't known what to expect, she'd gone with baggy pants under a full Abaya in blue with gold patterns worked in geometrically. The cloth around her head was an Amira hijab because of the embroidery around the edges, but she'd been wearing it Niqab-style to cover the lower half of her face.

That way, Nathaniel could recognize her, and probably nobody else.

He'd been ogling the girl's ass as she shopped for

flavors, then turned beet red when he saw her watching. Then white as a sheet as his brain engaged.

Hollyanne winked, just to watch him flinch a little, then went back to her phone that she had supposedly been reading while she relaxed.

Nathaniel seemed to relax as well. He didn't say anything. Or scream. Or run.

All good signs. Now, if they could only figure out what role the woman filled.

They had the awkwardness of a date. Second date, maybe, because both had been a little more relaxed than a first one always was.

Hollyanne could speak from experience on that. Lots of men out there that ogled her. Maybe wanted to be around her fame.

Few of them ever got up at first light and reminded themselves that they had to outwork everybody else today.

That was what it took to be Pacific Force.

Hollyanne shifted an arm enough to touch the baton she had under her Abaya. So many things you could hide with such an immensity of flowing cloth. The dark-skinned shop owner had looked at her a little askance until she spoke Persian to him, then he had lit right up and over-scraped her cup full of yumminess.

Not a lot of Iranians around here. Lots of Turks, but they'd been in West Germany a lot longer.

She listened as Nathaniel and woman were next in line. He spoke in a normal tone she remembered from other adventures. The woman was English. They'd been whispering to each other in English before switching to German to order.

Not exactly a date. Not exactly a bodyguard. Not exactly a minder.

"Hollyanne, this is Jake," he said over the earpiece

hidden under her Niqab. "Say hmmmm if everything is good right now."

She hummed and scrolled the article she'd been ignoring, instead tracking Nathaniel and the woman as they got served then paid.

The table right in front of her opened up and Hollyanne watched Nathaniel maneuver the tall woman so her back was to Hollyanne and he was facing both women.

Without the bodyguard, Hollyanne would have walked right up to the man and said something. As it was, she wasn't sure how Nathaniel intended to play this.

Still, she could wait. He knew she was here, and that boy was smart enough to understand that she wasn't alone.

CHAPTER
EIGHTEEN

NATHANIEL CONCENTRATED on his ice cream, happy that nervousness about asking Lady Nyx out on what might be construed as a real date could cover all the other emotional turmoil roiling beneath his skin. Didn't help when Hollyanne had winked at him.

Still, she was definitely a match for Lady Nyx if it came to that. Probably better, because Amanda had carried her gun in her purse, where she would have to get to it first. Hollyanne would pounce on her like a bobcat taking down a wolf. And win.

He studied this woman that his mind kept wanting to call Amanda. Separate her from the twin-gun killer in black leather named Lady Nyx. Maybe find him a way out of here that didn't look like a betrayal. Not when he might actually want to call her later and have her not immediately hang up on him. Or send killers his way.

She'd gotten a blueberry cobbler something, with berries, granola, and ice cream in a cup like his. He didn't feel like trying to eat a cone when he was pretty sure he'd end up wearing it.

Never take a first date to dinner. Nobody looks impressive when eating. Coffee first, though he didn't figure they could count that first operation as a date.

Or this one, when Nathaniel was pretty sure she might be willing to punch him in the face in a few minutes. Or shoot him.

Still, she had a cup of ice cream in one hand, the little wooden spoon in the other, and her purse was tucked in by her foot where it would be awkward to get to if Lady Nyx decided she needed her gun.

Nathaniel waited until they were about halfway finished before he spoke. More relaxed. More time to stare at a beautiful woman before she was angry at him.

Okay, maybe he was a little bit of a coward on that topic.

Still, Lady Nyx. Smart, beautiful, and dangerous. Pushed all his buttons.

"I have a weird question for you, Amanda," he said finally in English, channeling his *Dave* persona.

She looked up expectantly, ice cream on the corner of her mouth in the cutest way.

Steel blue eyes he could fall into forever.

"The boss has a few plans coming up," Nathaniel continued, speaking normally but aware that Hollyanne Kadjar was listening right behind the woman. And listening to both of them.

"That's right," Lady Nyx agreed, slowing her hands to study him. Looking for a clue.

"What happens after that whatever it is?" he asked. "We all go our separate ways, or is he planning something much more long-term that requires this level of staffing?"

"There will be immediate repercussions," she said. "Angry people. Being on the inside at that point will be smart because that will be the only safe spot."

"Sure, short term," Nathaniel nodded. "But I have a

phone number in London for you. I'd like to be able to call it sometime. Have you answer. Be happy to hear from me."

"You talk like you won't be around," she said, coming to that specific kind of stillness that only the best killers embodied.

Like the woman exactly behind her.

"At some point, I'd like to not be," Nathaniel said carefully, enunciating each syllable with precision. "I'm not really cut out to be a minion in somebody else's organization. Not after being my own boss for so long. I'm not sure the boss would let me just walk away."

Something changed in her eyes. Took him a moment to place it.

Amanda was gone. Lady Nyx was thinking about reaching into her bag and drawing a pistol.

"Why are you telling me this?" she asked in a much harder voice than a moment ago.

"Because I've been giving a lot of thought to things," he admitted. One hundred percent honest, too. Lots of might-have-beens. "I don't know enough to stop the current set of things he has planned. Haven't tried to find out, either. But I don't want to work for the man anymore."

"You're serious," she said.

Nathaniel watched her specifically *not move*, but he could see the woman's entire balance had shifted. Enough to punch him across the tiny table. Or dive into her bag and draw out his death.

Small ice cream shop. Nowhere to run. Hollyanne could save him. Would she?

"I am," Nathaniel replied, committing himself. "I'd like to finish my ice cream, walk out that door behind me, and vanish."

"Why are you telling me this?" she demanded in a deadly, quiet rasp.

"Because you could stop me," he told her. "Or you could let me go."

He paused to take a breath.

"Or you could come with me."

Something happened in those steel-blue eyes, but he didn't know her nearly well enough to identify which of the Stages of Death she'd landed on.

"Come with you?" she pressed awkwardly. "You can't just walk away. Not from something like this. He'll hunt you."

"I'm aware of that," Nathaniel said. "This wasn't the spur of the moment thing on my part. They never are."

"All that planning," she breathed. "You were gaming all this out?"

"I was," Nathaniel nodded. "How I could get out. Why I would rather you escort me than that crazy bitch with the knife fetish. She couldn't stop me, but I wouldn't want her phone number. What I would like is your help, at a dead minimum. And your understanding, though I might not get it. You are the last person in that building I would want to betray, because you are the most dangerous. And the only one I would like to talk to again. But I can't stay. Won't stay. Must go."

He could see her mind already reaching for the gun and wondered if Hollyanne would have to intervene. Lady Nyx hadn't moved, though.

Frozen, like another of Medusa's victims.

"So you can watch me go, Amanda," he continued. "Or stop me."

He paused for a long moment as he listened to her breathe.

"Or join me."

HOLLYANNE DIDN'T DO romance books. Or that one cable channel that started showing Christmas romance movies in August. Nevertheless, she knew the genre.

And would have lost any bet ever about seeing Nathaniel Hoestler walk himself into that sort of scene.

At least he'd picked a deadly woman to seduce.

Hollyanne had watched this Amanda chick move and knew that she was trouble. Not a lot of martial arts training, but deadly nonetheless.

Looked like she was Nathaniel's minder after all. Hollyanne hoped that the microphone might be strong enough to pick up the conversation, but she doubted it. And couldn't really say anything right now without tipping Amanda over into a bad place.

Hollyanne assumed a weapon in the oversized purse. It hung heavy. Several pounds of gun heavy. And Nathaniel had told Amanda she could stop him if she wanted.

Hollyanne had seen Nathaniel and Jake go toe-to-toe in close combat not that long ago, and Jake was better than just about anybody she knew.

Just about.

So gun. In expert hands, Hollyanne had to presume.

Jake and the others were outside the shop, watching and waiting, but wouldn't make entry until they had a positive signal from her. A Niqab had been the only way to make sure she wasn't immediately recognized in here.

Nathaniel talked. Hollyanne and Amanda both listened, but for different reasons. Hollyanne wanted to know if the woman would take Nathaniel up on his offer. There was a lot of subtext floating around, but something bad was in the offing and Nathaniel wanted out beforehand.

Amanda wasn't so sure.

Hollyanne sat perfectly still as Nathaniel concentrated on Amanda.

Finally, he reached that emotional peak. The point in the conversation where the cowboy has to ride off into the sunset.

Amanda seemed frozen in indecision.

Nathaniel waited a five-count, then slid his chair back noisily with a nod. Forcing the issue. Hollyanne's chair was already back enough to stand because she'd lucked into the last one of the four.

She rose like a blue ghost exiting an icy corpse. Nathaniel never once looked at her, instead having eyes only for Amanda.

"What will it be?" he asked Amanda quietly.

As far as breakups went, this one had to be in the top five she'd ever witnessed. Usually, her own relationships kind of faded out, mostly because she never stayed in one place for too long and most men couldn't really handle an independently wealthy woman who didn't give a shit what they thought.

Hollyanne watched the woman's head. Long hair down past her shoulders in a dark chocolate, almost black. It would rotate up and to her left to get to her purse and her gun. That would be when Hollyanne struck.

Blindside.

"He'll kill you," Amanda whispered up to Nathaniel.

"He's welcome to try," Nathaniel answered. "Better men have failed."

"Just like that?" she asked.

"For you," he nodded, still ignoring Hollyanne's ghost to focus on Amanda. "For me, it started a while ago when I asked what kind of world we'd live in if men like him were successful. I don't want that. Most people don't, which is why they are doing this the way they are. Going to burn the world down before anybody can stop them."

"And you intend to stop him?" Amanda demanded in a hard, quiet voice. "You really think you can?"

"I do," Nathaniel said quietly, nodding to her. "And I have friends who will help me. I'd like you to be one of them."

Okay, that was a low blow. Nathaniel must really have feelings for this woman. Hollyanne had never even heard of him being like this, and they'd captured almost all of his peons at one time or another. But then, all of his previous gang had been male, too.

Worse, Nathaniel was apparently counting on her and Jake helping him take down whoever Amanda's boss was, in whatever nefarious scheme that man had cooked up.

Assuming Hollyanne didn't have to take down Amanda right now.

Must be pretty damned bad.

Amanda hung in frozen indecision.

"Please?" Nathaniel asked the woman.

It was a good thing Hollyanne's Niqab was back up covering her mouth, because it fell open as he said that, extending a hand to the woman.

Amanda just sat there, then something broke in her. Hollyanne wasn't sure what, but the woman didn't immediately dive for the expected gun in the purse. Instead, she reached out a hand and took Nathaniel's, like two strangers meeting in an ice cream shop and shaking.

"Okay," Amanda whispered so quietly that Hollyanne barely heard it.

Still, it was enough.

Nathaniel tugged the woman to her feet, at which point Amanda turned enough to realize that she was boxed entirely in by a pair of close-combat experts that could have neutralized her gun.

Hollyanne watched Amanda's eyes get big.

"You," she whispered.

Smart woman, she didn't make any sudden moves that got her punched in the face or stomach. Helped that Nathaniel was holding her hand, anchoring the woman somewhat in place where she couldn't lunge for the gun in the purse.

Amanda got control of herself in a single heartbeat, then grinned.

"Wow," she muttered. Then turned back to Nathaniel. "How did you do that?"

One thumb did come up to indicate Hollyanne, but nothing else.

"I will tell you later," Nathaniel said. "For now, we need to go. Hollyanne, could you grab her purse?"

Amanda flinched, but thought better of it, realizing that all of Pacific Force was here, plus Nathaniel. And she had chosen Nathaniel's side, apparently.

Not hers and Jake's, but not whoever it was who had scared Nathaniel into calling his worst enemies in the world for help.

Nathaniel turned and pulled Amanda's hand into the

crook of his elbow, like two lovers on a date. The woman resisted for a moment, then shifted her entire body language with a nod and fell in with him.

Hollyanne squatted to grab the heavy bag without taking her eyes off the lovebirds, confirming the weight of a pistol in it as she did. Nathaniel led them towards the door. Hollyanne stood and slung the purse over her shoulder.

"Rik, we're exiting," Hollyanne said in a conversational voice. "Three of us."

"Three?" Rik asked, the sound of the engine gunning in the background.

"That's right."

JAKE WAS RIDING IN BACK, next to the woman known for today as Amanda, with Hollyanne on the far side. Nathaniel was up front. Grant and Spencer were in a trailing sedan, watching for people watching the truck.

Amanda seemed utterly gobsmacked by the turn of events.

Jake turned to study her.

"Do you have a passport on you good enough to cross Schengen Convention borders?" he asked the beautiful stranger.

That set of agreements and treaties allowed free movement within the EU, minus only the UK, who seemed intent on leaving anyway, as soon as they could somehow manage to get their shit together.

Assuming they could.

"I do," she nodded, a little breathless.

"Good," Jake said, "because we're flying under the radar here, having crossed the channel on a yacht belonging to a friend and bribing a few officials to take their time entering information into the computer system. Obviously, we can't smuggle you all the way back into

Britain without a little effort, but we'll figure something out."

He watched her eyes. Hollyanne had given him a hand signal that the woman seemed safe, but also had pulled a Beretta 93R out of her purse and cleared it of ammunition before putting it back.

Only professionals and lunatics needed a 93R to do things, and Jake wasn't sure which one Amanda could be classified as just yet.

"Nathaniel, how tight are we for time?" Jake asked, turning to his oldest friend among the six of them, and worst enemy, once Nathaniel had chosen a different life from the rest of them.

"A week," the man said. "The man in charge here in Bonn won't panic about us until we miss a check-in in about three hours, at which time they'll go into a hard lockdown and maybe start to run. I don't have all the details, so either Amanda does or we'll need to hit his base."

"Who is *he*?" Hollyanne asked as Rik accelerated out of the neighborhood.

There was a hotel out on the edge of town, dating back to the needs of traveling bureaucrats when this was the West German capital. A little long in the tooth now, but out of the way and nice.

"He calls himself *Lord Wraith*," Nathaniel replied. "Think comic book villain in costume and all that. He's planning a Kessler event somehow with a launch in the next week to ten days. Sometime soon. It will be bad."

Kessler? Shit.

Science fiction loved the idea because it was such a Frankenstein's Monster kind of scenario. Named after American NASA scientist Donald Kessler, when he originally realized that there was already too much junk in Low

Earth Orbit, all the way back in 1978, and that it was only going to get worse over time.

The Event itself would begin when something broke up and fragments started impacting other satellites, destroying them in turn and filling LEO with so much debris that it cascaded worse and worse, blowing up more and more satellites until everything was destroyed.

Worse, it would take decades of no more launches, if it got that bad, for enough junk to fall due to atmospheric drag for it to be really safe to try to launch something as fragile as a rocket again. Weather satellites. Communications. Everything at lower levels would be destroyed, leaving only things already way up there in geosynchrous orbit to survive, where they would eventually die of old age.

"Spencer, start looking up Kessler Syndrome Events and get me some solid background information by the time we get to the hotel," Jake said aloud. Grant was driving back there, so he could. "Call people if you have to. Also, get me a list of every orbital rocket launch planned, whoever and wherever, over the next four weeks."

"On it," Spencer said in his ear.

Jake turned to Amanda now.

"Do you know how Lord Wraith is planning to do it?" he asked.

She shrank in on herself a little as he scowled down on her, but all her height was in her legs, so sitting she was barely bigger than Hollyanne.

"No," she answered quietly.

It had been a long-shot. If Nathaniel didn't know, there might not be many people in the organization who did, because that meant it was probably in this Lord Wraith's head.

Jake nodded to the woman. Tried to smile, mostly because Hollyanne was treating her as at least neutral.

"Are we being tracked?" Rik asked from the driver's seat. "Electronically?"

"I've disabled this one," Nathaniel answered, holding up a much-battered cell phone. "Hollyanne, could you see if Amanda has one and set it to airplane mode? Better, just dump everything out and we'll chuck the bag itself, just in case."

"Why the bag?" Amanda asked, face screwed up in confusion.

"Easiest place to hide a tracking bug," Nathaniel answered. "When we get someplace, we should lose the clothes for the same reason. Jake, can I borrow something? It will fit. Rik's stuff might be a bit baggy on Amanda, but that will work for now as well."

"Can do," Jake answered. "Spencer, do you have anything that will identify a transmitter?"

"Back here with me," he said. "You want to pull over somewhere, Rik?"

"There's a boulevard with street parking coming up," she said. "Meet us there."

Jake leaned back and nodded.

You could never be too careful in this game. If Nathaniel was nervous, they all should be.

Especially if they had to turn right back around and stage a raid on some base where this Lord Wraith was hiding.

TWENTY-ONE

HOLLYANNE ENDED up with Spencer's gadget. Which was good, because it beeped twice when scanning Amanda. Her jacket had something sewn into a seam that was pinging every ten seconds. That was easy enough to handle.

It was the one in her bra that the boys would have had a hard time dealing with.

Hollyanne let the device rest right in the center, where the two underwires would cross.

"Son of a bitch!" Amanda muttered under her breath as her bosom beeped. "Really?"

Hollyanne shrugged and shared a commiserating smile with the woman.

Somebody had known what they were doing. If you had a good bra, you'd take care of it. Never lose it. Maybe not notice when somebody added a small electronic device in it to track you whenever you went because the fit of every bra constantly evolved over any four-week-period.

Amanda's jacket was already in the front seat with Nathaniel's blazer, itself possessed of two transmitters, one in a button and one in the shoulder pad.

Amanda had to squirm a little to reach the hook in back, but Hollyanne wasn't about to offer to help, nor was Jake from the look in his eyes. Instead, everybody watched the performance as the woman twisted inside her T-shirt, withdrawing first one arm and then the other before her lacy, white bra emerged and got handed forward.

Amanda leaned back and crossed her arms defensively across her chest. Hollyanne didn't blame her, so she popped off her Abaya and gave it to the stranger to wear. Hollyanne had pants and a thick shirt underneath.

Plus, she still had her armored sports bra underneath.

Amanda had a shirt just barely thick enough to hide anything. Maybe.

"Spencer, just lose those," Jake ordered. "In that trashcan or something."

Hollyanne noted the direction Jake was pointing and nodded. Edge of a park, so maybe it would look on a screen like the two lovebirds had taken a bus to the park and were sitting on one of the nearby benches or something.

And lovebirds was *absolutely* the term Hollyanne would use, even if she was certain they had never done more than hold hands before walking into that ice cream store.

Something about jumping off a ledge together.

"He didn't trust us at all?" Amanda demanded. Of Nathaniel apparently, because the other three of them might as well have not been in the truck as Rik started driving again.

"Would you?" Nathaniel countered with a shrug. "He's into his endgame, whatever it is. I'm a newcomer and have asked to go on an unnecessary field trip into the city at a bad time. Even accompanied by his deadliest assassin, he's got to assume that something might happen to me. To us.

Maybe my enemies show up and I'm arrested. Or yours. Maybe no less than Pacific Force itself is suddenly in town and about to ruin everything. The question then is not paranoia, but sufficient paranoia for survival. That's why I cracked open both phones and pulled the batteries in addition to airplane mode. I would like to vanish off the face of the earth, at least long enough to stop this madman."

"Which brings me to the next interesting crisis," Jake broke in before the lovebirds got going. "Nathaniel, I'm assuming that you would like to make us a deal whereby our two sides team up to stop Lord Wraith, after which you'd expect to go free?"

"Yes, Jake," Nathaniel said, turned as far as he could be with the seat belt holding him. "This is world-shattering in scope. Bring down civilization or at least cause a catastrophe that makes the Great Depression look like ants at a Sunday picnic. I could have stayed silent and watched it happen, but I don't want men and women like that destroying the world. Do you have any idea how hard it would be to take over everything if they burned it down first?"

Hollyanne suppressed a snort.

Nathaniel had never been about taking over the world, so she presumed he was putting on a performance for Amanda. Playing in the big leagues, when he'd always been more comfortable hiding in the third or fourth tier of villains, making his money from his various scams while not being high enough on anybody's radar that they sent strike teams or missile drones after him.

Hollyanne didn't have the heart to tell the man that he might have been better off just founding some tech start-up down in Santa Clara and becoming a billionaire that way. There were a lot of them, and most were far worse psychopaths than Nathaniel ever dreamed of being.

Jake had nailed it earlier. Both Nathaniel and Pacific Force played by rules. Not necessarily laws, but those men in the billionaire class—and they were almost all men—seemed to skirt every law they could sue or ignore to evade.

Part of the reason the world was so fragile now. Too many chiselers. Too many beavers gnawing away at the roots of the system for their own advantage, and screw everybody else.

"Well, we've rescued you, so that's step one," Jake said. "When we get to the hotel, you'll need to brain dump everything you have so we can figure out how to stop this guy. Will we need to go in there with heavy firepower? Because we were operating in the dark, and crossing several countries, we didn't bring hardly anything with us for a tactical assault."

"I can get you guns," Amanda spoke up. "Today. Here in Bonn. We'll have to move quickly, if you want to do that then turn around and attack Lord Wraith, but I have connections we could call."

"Does he know who they are?" Hollyanne asked the woman.

"I don't think so," Amanda replied, turning to face her. "Lord Wraith is mostly charisma and brains running a cult, rather like your President. Folks come to him armed. I have had to make sure I had access to some underworld armorers on the side for my Berettas and other armaments because there was nobody inside who impressed me."

"You'll talk to Grant when we get there, then," Hollyanne decided, glancing over to get a nod from Jake. "He's the face man of the group, so he'll know them or will deal with them for arms later."

Amanda nodded. At least she was acting like a team

player, even if she was as close to being under arrest as you could get without handcuffs.

Everybody turned back to Nathaniel now.

"Jake, the man must be stopped," he said. "I'd rather not go back to prison, but if that's the trade-off, I'll deal with it and figure out a way to escape later. Like last time."

"You feel that strongly, Nathaniel?" Jake asked.

"I do."

"Then you better have one hell of a good story when we get to the hotel."

CHAPTER
TWENTY-TWO

NATHANIEL HAD DONE IT. He didn't want to say it out loud, but convincing Jake and the others to help had always been the hardest part in his mind. Lord Wraith was a former punk musician with delusions of grandeur and one hell of an operations budget that had come from... *somewhere.*

The killers he had hired, once you got beyond Lady Nyx, were all third rate. Grim Motoko, Dead Eve, Neon Scoundrel. All of them, near as Nathaniel had been able to tell without seeing them naked, were women.

Had all this gone beyond a simple crime gang and turned into cult? Why else hire so many women—and only women—in positions of deadliness? Shit, were they all supposed to be his groupies?

Ick.

But everyone was at the hotel. In a private suite. Lady Nyx had taken his hand getting out of the truck and squeezed it as Jake had led them inside, boxed in by the others as they walked.

Coffee.

He hadn't made it to their coffee date, but she'd taken the offer of some as well.

Hell of a first date. Hopefully, the first of many, but he had to save the world first.

Hollyanne would never let him live it down. If they ever found out, nor would any of his former gang later..Jake, at least, just grinned knowingly.

Lady Nyx got introduced to everybody as Amanda for now. They probably assumed a costumed identity for her, but it was no more real than Amanda. Hell, Nathaniel didn't even know her real name.

Spencer was talking.

"The bad news first," he said. "Everybody seems to have at least one launch scheduled for the period in question. Governmental and civilian. US civilian, NASA, ESA, JSA, Russians, Chinese. Even the Indians are planning to launch a new communications satellite."

"Get me phone numbers of the associated decision makers," Jake ordered. "Either we're successful with this raid and know who to call, or I need to call everybody and convince them to scrub until they can crack open their payloads and confirm it. That will be expensive, and we'll end up owing favors or making enemies, at least until someone discovers a bomb. Nathaniel, any idea how he plans to do it?"

"When I asked, and mind you I didn't press too hard because I was already on thin ice with those folks, he said ball bearings," Nathaniel answered. "Enough to trigger a cascade. Blow up a hollow shell and scatter a cloud of them?"

"That or maybe a full payload of boobytrapped cube-sats," Spencer said. "You could deploy those more evenly and have them work their way out all over the place before subsequently exploding and making a freaking mess up there."

"How do we clear the skies if he pulls it off?" Nathaniel asked, looking at everyone.

Again, one of those topics you did NOT research while in the middle of an enemy base about to do such a thing.

"Wait fifty years and hope enough have come down that you are safe," Spencer replied. "Ten years might be safe, but the risk starts high and only goes down arithmetically every year. People have also talked about using high energy lasers. You heat up one side of an object. If you are lucky, that changes its orbit and makes it hit the atmosphere sooner. From the ground, it will take a while, because you need a lot of energy and are functionally doing advanced research on new energy weapons that everybody will want to use later. If you can get something into orbit, the tech we've got now would be good enough. Still would take years, but once you start cleaning out one level, you can work up or down and get the rest. Eventually, it will be clear. Again, years or decades."

"Fuck," Nathaniel muttered. The others agreed.

Lady Nyx was still holding his hand. She squeezed it and that really helped.

He'd asked her to risk everything without any understanding. And she had.

He couldn't let her down.

Instead, he turned to the white board that Jake, or probably Spencer, carried everywhere. On it, Nathaniel started plotting a rough map of the compound. It helped that the place had started as a warehouse and all the walls been built later. Almost no outside windows looking over the parking lot or side spots where pallets of stuff or truck trailers had probably been parked, once upon a time.

"You've got a chain link fence all the way around,

topped with three strands of barbed wire," Nathaniel explained as he wrote. "It is not wired with alarms, because that was on my list of things to do next year. Assuming we still needed the facility. Doors are wired and coded to keycards. Those are easy enough to spoof. Grant, if you have some gear, I can get you the frequencies and the challenge codes for the overrides."

Grant nodded and reached into a briefcase nearby. Nathaniel understood how Grant worked. Often, you could talk your way in, but sometimes you had to pick a lock. Mechanical or electronic instead of social.

"Inside, you have offices here," Nathaniel sketched more. "Barracks for goons in these two spots and for officers like me and Amanda here. Lord Wraith maintains a full suite back in this corner, but I've never been beyond his office at the front here to know what he has for personal use beyond."

He turned to Amanda unconsciously. Watched her turn beet red at a question he hadn't asked.

At the same time, Lord Wraith had hired female killers. All of them, if you assumed Neon Scoundrel had been Assigned Female At Birth, regardless of her current proclivities and androgynous appearance.

"No," she replied quietly, answering that question unasked. "Only the office up front."

Nathaniel nodded and smiled. Win or lose, the two of them were in this together, unless he could talk Jake into letting her walk free when he went back to prison.

Burn that bridge when he got there.

"So timing will be the key here," Nathaniel continued. "We have a check-in in two hours eighteen minutes. If the op was running normal, we'd already be back and checked in by the folks at the door. If not, we'd call with certain codewords indicating the issue, but the fact that we'd called would have already triggered an alert. Depending on Lord Wraith's mood, maybe he jumps in a car and bolts. Maybe he locks everything down and prepares to go out in a blaze of glory. Either way, there is a serious risk that he burns all the computer systems to erase evidence and any clues we might use, with the rest in his head and I'm pretty sure nothing short of torture would get him to spill in time."

"Ticking bomb scenario," Jake nodded.

At least Nathaniel was working with professionals. This had been one of the things about Lord Wraith that had left him cold and nervous. It wouldn't have been as bad, had they looked like the folks who would know how to handle the world after they'd broken it.

Instead, they'd struck him like children playing with matches for the most part.

"Basically," Nathaniel answered. "We've got to do this fast and heavy or burn a lot of national astronautics agencies annual budgets with scrubbed launches. Plus, Lord Wraith was paid to do this. Not the South African billionaire nutcase who thinks he's the world's greatest genius, but one of that man's enemies. Another billionaire who is losing or already has lost the space race so they decided to flip the whole game board over instead."

"Is that evidence in the computers?" Jake asked.

"I didn't dig, for obvious reasons, but there's a lot of money floating around," Nathaniel nodded. "It had to come from somewhere, so all I'd need is a bank account number and I can get you that. And maybe clean Lord Wraith out completely so he's no longer a threat later."

"Seed money for your next venture?" Jake teased, but Nathaniel was deadly serious.

"I'm not an anarchist, Jake," he retorted sharply. "Criminal mastermind, sure. Lawless pain in the ass at times? Fine, I'll own that, too. But this was too much. This is a dumbass destroying the world in a fit of infantile, ego-driven pique. Several of them, if you look at the layers of assholes involved. Personally, I think all those shits should be taken down a few notches because they've apparently decided that they are more important than governments and everyone else. How long until the next punk decides to do something equally monumentally stupid?"

"Who are you and what have you done with Nathaniel Hoestler?" Jake asked. Serious, but a gleam of wicked laughter in his eyes. And respect.

"I found a line I won't cross, Jake," Nathaniel said, turning to make eye contact with everyone in here, including Lady Nyx, if she'd had any doubts as to who he was before she walked into this hotel room. "Is that enough for the rest of you, or do I need to call some of my old chums and her people and see if we can do this alone?"

"Oh, I'm in," Jake said. The others assented loudly as well. "I just never imagined having this conversation with you."

"You aren't the only one, Jake," Nathaniel nodded. "Trust me on that. I had to spend several days thinking about it and really meeting Wraith's people before it crystallized. I asked Amanda to come out with me because the rest of them are junior varsity spearchuckers, as far as I'd rate them. But for them being armed lunatics with automatic weapons, you and Hollyanne could take them all down yourselves, probably. I need Lord Wraith taken down and in custody before he manages to destroy my evidence and my future."

Jake nodded and turned to Amanda now, just as serious.

"This is where you are in, or out," Jake said sternly.

Lady Nyx shivered. Hell, Nathaniel almost shivered from that tone. From the implications.

But Lady Nyx recovered quickly. Glanced at Nathaniel and he smiled at her.

"Call Gerhardt," she said to Grant, adding a local telephone number. "Leave a message and introduce yourself as a friend of Sabine. Ask him to call you back at that number about an order of fish."

Nathaniel and Jake both turned to Grant, but the man was already dialing.

She was in. He was in. Pacific Force was in.

Would it be enough?

TWENTY-THREE

JAKE HAD SENT GRANT, Rik, and Amanda into one of the sleeping chambers while he, Nathaniel, and Hollyanne were out in the main chamber. Spencer was heads-down in a corner doing research.

Everything was available on the internet if you had infinite time and patience to look. Plus perfect knowledge of which parts that you found were conspiracy theories and which were truths.

Jake had instincts and training, but very little time.

He turned to Nathaniel.

"Do you envision this as kick in the door and kill anything that moves?" he asked.

Nathaniel grimaced.

"It might come to that, Jake," he replied, so at least he was being honest. "Grant can defeat any keyfob door we come to with the codes I've given him, but at some point, we're going to run into folks that won't recognize you or Hollyanne, and they'll panic. I have no idea how deep into the facility we'll be at that point to tell you how it will have to go down. I'm hoping we can slip in like ninjas, grab that Russian moron and his laptop, and slip out without anyone being the wiser. At that point, German police and heavy teams can take down the rest by themselves."

"And if we fail to get the launch information?" Jake asked. "Do we end up calling everyone and asking them to scrub launches and look inside their rockets?"

"Honestly?" Nathaniel asked, so Jake nodded. "I can't come up with a better solution. Spencer said fourteen scheduled launches in the window, but I think the last six can be skipped, because the hint I got suggested the next week or so, not out a month."

"That leaves eight," Jake replied.

"I know."

Jake nodded. If Nathaniel could have handled it inside, he might have. That much was obvious from the look on his face right now. But there was that big distinction between criminals and anarchists. Back in junior high when he'd been into role-playing games, the difference between Lawful Evil and Chaotic Evil.

Jake turned to Hollyanne. She was bright-eyed.

"Do we just send Nathaniel and Amanda back in alone like nothing had happened?" he asked.

She was the close-combat tactical expert to his strategic planning.

She surprised him by turning to Nathaniel. Surprised Nathaniel, too.

"How emotionally involved is she?" Hollyanne asked. "For that matter, how about you? Remember, I was in the ice cream shop with you."

Nathaniel shrugged. Tossed his head back and forth.

"I asked her to walk off a cliff with me and she did," he replied. "I don't think she's as far along the path of saving the world as I am, but I also don't think she's a deep sleeper agent sent to keep me in line. If she is, we're fucked. The world is fucked."

"I agree with you," Hollyanne said. "She's looking for something from you. Dunno if it is romance or a promotion beyond bush league villainy, but that's also beyond the scope of today. Would you trust her with a live Beretta, walking back into Lord Wraith's base, prepared to kill people for no better reason that one of us told her to?"

Jake blinked. That was about as raw as it got.

And it took him back to the old RPG alignment charts. You could negotiate with Nathaniel. The man had surrendered to them twice rather than getting himself killed. Both times he had subsequently escaped the British.

There was always tomorrow, as long as you weren't dead. Did Amanda understand that?

"I think so," Nathaniel said after a moment of thought.

"Too bad neither Rik nor I could impersonate her, at least for a bit," Hollyanne laughed. "We'll just have to trust that you're at least as charming as you like to think of yourself, Nathaniel."

He started to rise to the bait, then caught himself with a wry smile.

"I have missed having people good enough to tease me," he replied.

"You could always change your ways," Jake said.

Nathaniel shook his head ruefully.

"Pretty sure it's too late for me," he said. "Too many governments would still want to put me in prison forever, even if I had a complete Road to Damascus moment here. And it is kinda sad that my worst enemies in the world turned out to be the only people I trusted most when it came down to this. Thank you for listening. For helping. I may not get a chance to say that later, and I want you to understand it now."

Jake held out a hand and Nathaniel gripped it like a life preserver in rough seas. Then Hollyanne wrapped the bigger man up in a tremendous hug.

Not many people could even understand that comment, let alone appreciate it. Nathaniel Hoestler's evil had really been the catalyst that caused Pacific Force to come into being. Nineteen years later, they were all back to that day in early 1998 when Nathaniel had walked away from them the first time.

What a road we've all walked in twenty years…

Nathaniel almost seemed on the verge of tears when he made eye contact with Jake. They shared a nod that seemed to say everything.

Just as well, because as Hollyanne stepped back, the door to the bedroom opened and Rik emerged first, followed by Grant and Amanda.

"We're a go," she said simply.

Jake nodded. Weapons were covered if she was that confident.

Now, they just had to freelance their way inside an enemy stronghold, capture a dragon, and steal his hoard of gold in order to save the world.

Just another day in the life of Pacific Force.

THEY CALLED HER AMANDA, mostly because that had been the cover identity she had assumed when escorting Moriarty, the infamous Nathaniel Hoestler, outside the compound. When she couldn't be Lady Nyx, the deadly assassin.

In many ways, it almost felt like being born again. Offered a second chance to make a whole new set of interesting mistakes as an adult, having learned so much from the teenage exuberance of being the disowned daughter of an English Baron, a third child who would never inherit anything except connections to other second scions.

And maybe a bit of a rebellious streak that had carried her into some dark and interesting places.

A hotel suite outside Bonn, surrounded by Pacific Force, had never been anywhere on her list. Worse, she was about to help them take down her current—former already?—employer, the anarchist Lord Wraith.

And she as looking forward to it. How weird was the rest of the day going to get?

Rik Farrell was the firearms expert. She'd already take

the Beretta apart, cleaned it, and reassembled it flawlessly. Faster than Amanda could have.

Maybe she should just keep being Amanda? Leave off Sabine Kingston entirely, once she was done with Gerhardt and the team was armed?

New woman, new mistakes?

Moriarty wasn't going straight, regardless of the situation. He wanted to conquer the world instead of destroying it. Amanda wasn't as sure, but she also knew who was going to win this battle.

Lord Wraith had charisma and money. Moriarty had deadly friends. Including Lady Nyx.

Weird.

Amanda turned to Farrell as the tall, busty blonde handed her the weapon.

"I'd have somebody check the sere spring at some point," the woman said seriously. "It's not bad yet but feels a little off."

All that from just popping it open? Not firing it?

But then, Pacific Force was famous. A team of five experts who had their own comic book in addition to everything else. Rik Farrell was supposedly the best firearms expert on the West Coast.

Amanda nodded and tucked the gun into a small messenger bag, along with both spare clips of ammunition and one in the grip. She could draw, chamber, and fire in one smooth motion, but doing do right now might send the wrong signal to the others.

They were all watching her a little more closely than probably necessary, but the rest had known each other for over twenty years, if rumors were to be believed.

"Thank you," Amanda said, turning to Jake McNeil. He and Moriarty were in charge.

"What the final tally?" Jake asked the blonde.

"About eight grand US," she replied. "Covering it out of petty funds right the moment, but I'm guessing there will be reward money for some of these jerks when we capture them."

"Good enough," the man said, turning to study Amanda's face now. "We're going to your armorer, then directly into battle. Anything you need to cover other than a pit stop now and possibly a second one when we get close?"

Amanda considered her options. She had committed. All in. If nothing else, it kept her out of jail immediately, because she had the impression that McNeil would have called someone to pick her up.

And Moriarty—she needed to think of him as Nathaniel—was convinced that they would be able to escape later.

She had no intention of going straight. If nothing else, her father the Baron and both older brothers had already disowned and denounced her over her criminal proclivities years ago. Cut her off entirely. And Nathaniel had asked if he could still call her phone number. That was more than mere recruiting.

At least she hoped so.

"No," Amanda replied, trying to find a way to shift her mind to include both Amanda and Lady Nyx, without any traces of Sabine Kingston.

She could never go back to that woman. That life. Those fucked up teenage years and all the things she'd done.

But Nathaniel and Pacific Force had offered her a way out forward.

If she had the guts to run with it.

This was the brass ring. The big leagues.

She could finally be somebody in her own right, rather than the child of somebody.

HOLLYANNE DIDN'T KNOW who Amanda or Sabine was when she wasn't being Lady Nyx, but had a better understanding of why Nathaniel had been so intent on getting her to escape Lord Wraith when he did.

And not just because she might have shot him in the back when he tried.

Calm in the face of impending, massive violence. Expert with the pistol, just from the way she handled the weapon, even going so far as to put it away without racking a round first. Confident that she could in a pinch, without provoking anyone here. That had been the message in her eyes as Hollyanne watched.

Almost thirty, but not yet. Soon. Hollyanne remembered those last few years, arguing with her mother about grandkids Hollyanne wasn't interested in pursuing yet.

Ever?

Maybe. Maybe not. Of the team, only Grant had tried marriage. And was still failing at it, to hear his stories of ex-girlfriends who thought they could tame him.

Maybe that was it. No man would ever tell Hollyanne

Kadjar what to do, Jake notwithstanding when he was running an op. Never box her in with demands. With rules.

More than once, she and Jake had looked at each other like Nathaniel and Amanda did now, but never stepped across that line. Never walked off a cliff together.

Would they, one of these days? Would any of the five of them ever find someone and settle down, or had the whole thing evolved into a loose polycule? Five lives overlapping some but not fully.

Not today's problem. Today, they had to go stop some madman with big dreams and small understanding of the repercussions.

Jake looked around at everybody, that last minute check-in before things began to roll.

"We're going in hot," he said simply. "Grant, you let Nathaniel and Amanda lead until we run into a door they can't penetrate, then you take it out as rapidly as you can. Amanda, you'll have point-wing covering Nathaniel against anything coming at you from the front. We'll have your flanks covered until it comes time to rotate someone else up front. Rik will be in overwatch from the inside, since we don't have a way to use a sniper. Spencer will be her point-wing spotter as usual. Move fast. Bullshit anyone you can but expect to have to take someone down eventually. I'd prefer fists, because that is quieter and we have zip-ties and gags we can use for stealth, but eventually someone might open fire. Do not show mercy when they do. Anyone pointing a gun at us today dies. Am I clear?"

Hollyanne gulped, unused to Jake in this serious—this lethal—a mood. At the same time, she understood the need. Outsiders on both sides of the equation. Punk anarchists willing to burn the world down if allowed. Strangers working with the team.

They needed to get to Lord Wraith and find out what

he knew. Capture his files and read them, so they could quietly contact various folks and stop a rocket launching. Then go after whichever son of a bitch had decided to destroy the world.

Or maybe just let the governments involved handle it, however ineffectual they might be. They were likely to still be friendlier about the process than Jake and Nathaniel might be at that point, frightening as that concept sounded.

Amanda's reaction told Hollyanne how little actual combat the woman had seen. Mostly assassinations from a safe distance probably, like a drive-by or a sniper on a rooftop.

Not close enough that someone got their blood all over you when they died.

Everything Hollyanne had on could be washed to get the blood out. Occupational hazard in this business. Same with the rest of them.

Death wasn't common, but it was constant. At least they all had armor under their shirts now. Nathaniel wore a spare Jake had brought and Amanda had stuffed a spare T-shirt into one of Rik's spare vests, since she didn't have nearly the chest.

Time to go to work.

She nodded to Jake and followed him to the door.

TWENTY-SIX

NATHANIEL WONDERED if this might have been where he had ended up but for a moment of teenage anger that had split him off from the others twenty years ago. Except that without that, they might have turned into a corporation or a social club instead of mercenaries for justice.

Too late now to go back and redo it all. Best he had was the option to save the world today and slip out the side door while Jake and the others took all the credit. And they were welcome to it. The underworld didn't need to know how deeply involved Nathaniel had been.

Well, not true. There were always going to be more anarchists out there. Punks were fine. They were just pushing back against The Man and had been allies frequently because Nathaniel liked tweaking the System.

But not to burn it down.

Nobody won if everything was destroyed.

They climbed into the truck, with Nathaniel up front again, though Amanda was on the right behind him instead of in the middle. It was her contact. Rik drove. Grant and Spencer followed.

Bonn was a lovely town. Everything was green today as the drizzle came and went. Tourists and locals out for a bit of a pleasant late afternoon, unaware of how dangerous things were growing around them.

Calm waters hiding the monsters swimming below.

They crossed to a spot not far from the old government buildings. There was a gorgeous park nearby. Rik pulled to a curb and left the keys in the ignition as she and Amanda got out. Grant and Spencer had kept driving, presumably to circle around from the back in case there was trouble.

Blind meets in daylight were always a problem. West Germany had had all manner of terrorism problems back in the 70s and 80s, mostly Baader–Meinhof Group/Red Army Factions when the Western World had been lurching back to the right under Reagan and Thatcher. After Unification, they'd turned inward for a while, because the Soviets had also imploded and stopped funding so many revolutionary fronts and cells.

Seems they were back, from what Jake had mentioned earlier. Was Russia behind Lord Wraith, instead of one of the other billionaires? Nathaniel doubted that Lord Wraith had ever actually met the man funding him, whoever he was. Probably just interlocutionaries. Could have been fronting for anyone, as long as there was a big briefcase of cash handed over.

Or a pallet, in this case.

All the more reason to capture those files and that man, in order to find out the truth.

Save the world.

Nathaniel kept his grumbles to himself and watched the two women walk.

RIK WASN'T ENTIRELY comfortable with Amanda, but Jake and Hollyanne seemed to trust her. For now.

Enough to hand her a burst-capable machine pistol when nobody else was armed with a gun of any kind.

Amanda had laid out the meeting details and rules. Two of them, both women, one of whom was known to Gerhardt on sight. Cash. Brief chat in the park like old friends. Pick up a bag from the trunk of a nearby car when Gerhardt was satisfied.

Her shoulders kept itching like this was a drug deal or something. Cops, poised out of sight and ready to pounce as soon as they made contact for a buy.

Rik made a note to herself to establish a solid munitions base in Germany, or maybe France. In the old days, they operated out of England enough to have friends there they could call night or day for armaments, but the retirement of the team had thrown things off.

The rust was showing. She would need to up her game.

"There he is," Amanda murmured, leaning into Rik's shoulder and nodding towards a tall Viking on a park bench.

Long hair and hefty beard, somewhere darker than blond but not brown or gold. Ruddy chestnut, maybe. Smiling face. Shoulders that looked about a meter across. Felt like he'd be looking down on both of them when they got close.

Rik was five-eleven, and Amanda even taller. Gerhardt stood up as they got close, and Rik pegged him about six-foot-five. Huge.

Grinning, though.

"Sabine, so lovely to see you," he said as he lightly grabbed her upper arms and kissed her on the mouth. Friendly-like.

Then he turned her way and Rik felt his appraisal.

"Farrell?" he whispered, a bit taken back as his eyes got big.

Oh? Know Pacific Force on sight, do we?

But Rik supposed that underworld arms dealers might need to stay on top of things like that.

"Indeed," Rik answered. "Where's my kiss?"

She stepped up to the tall man and smiled. His kiss was more automatic and perfunctory than anything, but probably looked good enough if anybody was watching.

Gerhardt was certainly off-center as he stepped back and turned to Amanda.

"It's complicated," she said in that way that women can compress entire books into two words.

"Yes, I can imagine," Gerhardt replied. "Am I busted?"

"No," Amanda said. "I have, at least temporarily, changed sides, but I would appreciate you not mentioning that to outsiders. Rik and her friends are here to do something and needed weapons on extremely short notice. I thought of you."

"Thank you, I think," the man stumbled over his words.

Then he led them back to his bench and sat in the middle, as the plan originally called for. He was wearing a nice cologne today. Bright and a little citrusy, with just a hint of mint underneath. Suited him.

Gerhardt ignored Amanda for the moment.

"I'm equipping your team?" he asked, voice drawn out and up in awe.

"As she said, short notice and we need to kick in a door without calling in the police or the military."

"I see," he nodded. "Are you needing American flash/bang grenades? I always keep a couple in the car for emergencies."

"That would be helpful," Rik nodded. "We'd like to keep casualties to a minimum, but we're dealing with unsavory types."

"Like those Russians in Los Angeles?" he asked.

"You know about that?" Risk countered.

"It is a small industry, when you get right down to it," he nodded with a grin. "Almost incestuous that way. When Chechen mercs suddenly start offering heavy firepower for cheap, people notice. When Pacific Force comes out of retirement to stomp on them, that sends waves all through the harbor."

"We're back in business," Rik informed the man, watching his eyes get big again. "Pacific Force. We broke up an operation in Northern England a few months ago and have been working since then. I'm hoping that you might take our call if we find ourselves in a similar position later?"

Rik enjoyed the way his eyes blinked too rapidly. Amanda was watching but had remembered to close her mouth after a moment. At least before she caught any flies.

"I would be honored," Gerhardt managed.

How many criminal arms dealers, working under the

table, might be able to say that? Most of what the man did was probably legitimate. Record-keeping these days would keep too good a track on weapons moving around. You had to keep a second inventory of things *stolen* or *lost* along the way.

Presumably with the serial numbers filed off or maybe never stamped at the factory, depending.

Rik had a lot of experience with that sort of thing. And any number of friends, though mostly in the US or East Asia.

"So I have cash," Rik said, nodding to the man. "Would you like to see it here, or somewhere more private?"

He gave her a hard once over, then nodded to himself.

"I am willing to work on faith right now," he said, rising.

Rik joined him and they walked towards an edge of the park not all that far from where she'd left the truck.

"All pistols?" he asked, turning to Rik as they got close.

"We're penetrating a warehouse with armed guards and few doors," Rik answered. "You might hear about it tomorrow. Or not, depending on the government."

"I see," he offered.

Gerhardt opened the trunk to reveal a large duffel bag. Rik watched him unzip it and pull out a Sig Sauer P320 in a carry holster. Used enough to have some wear on the slide, but otherwise clean. Unloaded when he racked the slide open and handed it to her.

Rik kept it out of sight inside the trunk and worked the slide a few times. Well-oiled and smooth.

"How much ammunition do you have?" she asked him quietly.

"About five hundred rounds of 9mm," he said. "Got a

deal on the Sigs, so I have two spare magazines for each of the six you asked for."

"What do you want for the grenades?" she asked.

He studied her. It was completely different from those Chechen punks. Professionalism, which they'd had none of.

"Thousand US for both?" he asked.

"Deal," Rik answered.

Bit of a bargain on her part, but they were setting up for a longer-term relationship. Plus, he was making a nice profit on the Sigs already.

If they were all this well-maintained, she would definitely be sending him a Christmas card this year.

Rik reached into her back pocket and pulled out an envelope filled with hundred-dollar bills. Then reached into her other pocket for her wallet and pulled out ten more, handing them to him with a smile.

She looked around quickly but didn't see any cops suddenly rushing down to arrest her, which would have been rather embarrassing. Instead, she moved over to where she could see Jake in the truck, nodding to him.

Gerhardt opened a second bag, checked the contents, and slid them into the first with a grin. Rik zipped the bag up and lifted the mass, slipping the strap onto her shoulder.

"Tomorrow's news?" he asked carefully.

"Yup," Rik nodded.

"In that case, I might go visit my sister in Dusseldorf tonight," he grinned. "Get out of town for a bit, just in case the authorities are a bit put out for the rest of the week."

"That sounds like an excellent idea," Rik replied as the truck pulled up next to them. "We'll talk soon.

She opened the back door and slid in, Amanda hopping up behind her. Jake got back into motion with hardly any honking behind him.

"We good?" Nathaniel asked nervously from the front passenger seat.

Rather than explain, she opened a bag and handed him the Sig that was on top. She would need to touch the others before handing them out, but that first one was in good shape, and the rest looked it to the eyeball test.

"Time to find out," she replied, catching Jake's nod in the rear-view mirror.

CHAPTER
TWENTY-EIGHT

JAKE HAD the address and had studied it on various maps, including satellite images that just showed it as one of a series of warehouses in an industrial district on the outskirts of Bonn. Quiet. Self-contained. Close to a highway and rail options to haul things around.

Anonymous but for being the lair of a yahoo who called himself Lord Wraith.

Right now, they were parked about a mile away while the women got the firearms sorted. Turned out that Amanda was almost as good as Rik at that sort of thing.

Jake checked his watch and turned to Nathaniel.

"They going to panic soon?" he asked.

Nathaniel shrugged.

"Depends," he replied. "If they are watching the beacons, they think I am still in that park with Amanda, so that might make them nervous. Maybe panic. If I were to call in and say there was a problem, they would absolutely go into a hard lock-down. I still think that this is the best I can offer. Late afternoon so everyone's getting tired. Low sun so shadows. Not a lot of noise until we're inside and causing trouble. Hell, at that point I'd pull the fire alarms, but Lord Wraith had already disabled them earlier, figuring that having people die in a fire was better than having the fire department and cops ask questions about this many people living here full time."

Jake nodded. They'd chewed it around several times and several ways. Once Lord Wraith got nervous about Nathaniel, he might just run. Or burn all his files and vanish, leaving Jake to make a whole series of expensive phone calls.

Worth it, in the long run, assuming that this wasn't all some terrible snipe hunt. But expensive for everybody who didn't have a ticking bomb sitting on a rocket pad somewhere.

"Anybody in there you're going to miss if somebody has to shoot them?" Jake asked.

"She came out with me," Nathaniel answered with a wry grin. "Though right up to the last I wasn't sure Hollyanne wasn't going to have to tackle her."

"Serious?" Jake asked.

In the ten years they'd been chasing the man, Jake had heard no hint of a female involvement. But then, there weren't many folks you could trust in that industry, and Nathaniel had been focused mostly on recruiting his hooligans.

Nathaniel shrugged.

"Maybe," he said. "There was a moment, early on, but a lot of things have happened since then and I'm not sure where she is right now mentally. Won't know until we slip out the back later and make a run for Denmark or something. She might still shoot me then."

"I expect that we'll be busy with the German government for a while," Jake said, a sidelong notice that he wouldn't be chasing the man, nor setting the dogs after him.

Assuming all this was on the level.

"Thank you," Nathaniel replied. "I've been in my head a lot over this, Jake. The difference between crime and anarchy. New lines in the sand I would have never imagined even a year ago. Are we getting old?"

"Had that conversation with Grant in London last week," Jake chuckled. "Pacific Force might have to start recruiting some younger talent soon. Criminal masterminds don't have to maintain such punishing physical standards, though."

"I do if I want to keep her attention," Nathaniel chuckled back. "You haven't seen her in her main Lady Nyx costume. All black leather. Skintight. Distracting. Her daily workouts are at least three times as hard as mine, and I work at it."

Jake nodded.

It was weird, having this sort of a conversation with Nathaniel, but there honestly weren't many people in the world who would understand. You had to be in the business for a while to know the pressures and the problems.

Rik approached at that moment, a holstered pistol in each hand. She handed each of them a Sig.

"These are loaded and the safeties are on," she instructed them. "Seventeen plus one in the tube. Two spare magazines each, and all of us but Amanda can swap out on the fly. She'd staying with her Beretta for now. Everyone has ball ammunition so you should not have feed issues. However, one shot is not likely to kill someone, so you might plan for double-taps if you have to shoot. Plus, most vests will stop a 9mm ball at any range."

Jake nodded and took his, clipping it to the carrier to his belt. In all likelihood, he'd have it in hand for the entire stalk, as he had never worked to develop those quick-draw reflexes that cowboys had.

He turned to Nathaniel as Rik withdrew, leaving them alone.

"Thank you for calling," he said, holding out a hand.

Nathaniel took it.

"Thank you for answering."

NATHANIEL WAS in the front passenger seat while Rik drove the truck. Hollyanne, Jake, and Amanda across the back behind him. Poised for violence, but Nathaniel hadn't been able to find any other way.

Not enough time to uncover Lord Wraith's secrets without exposing himself. Not enough time to find out more about Lady Nyx. She might have decided to shoot him this afternoon.

And she might end up in London and take his call.

Weirder things had happened.

"This the place?" Rik asked as they approached an intersection.

"Yes," Nathaniel answered. "All the security cameras stop short of here and mostly focus on the front parking lot. Stupid, I know, but I've only been there a few months and the cybersecurity issues took higher precedence."

She grunted something that sounded rude, but he knew Rik was the team sniper. She'd normally be up on a nearby roof with a rifle or that damned bow of hers, usually with Spencer right next to her.

No way to do that today.

Still, she turned in and pulled to a stop. Grant was right behind her.

Everyone exited quickly and looked around, but it was late enough in the afternoon that folks had mostly headed home. Almost no operations around the clock in this business park.

Nathaniel reached back and touched the pistol on his hip with the heel of his hand. Mostly just a safety blanket kind of thing, because he was pretty sure everyone else here was a better shot.

That was why he'd had minions before. Being one sucked.

He turned to Amanda. Or Sabine. Or Lady Nyx.

Whoever she wanted to be.

She had lost her purse and her bra but had removed the covering Hollyanne had given her earlier and had the shirt out over her holster. He was wearing one of Jake's spare jackets, having transferred everything safely when he lost that nice blazer.

Hopefully, nobody had been paying that close attention earlier.

Plus, watching Amanda walk might distract folks at a critical moment.

She certainly did it to him.

"You ready?" he asked, holding out a hand.

She smiled and took it, squeezing tightly as she stepped up next to him.

"All eyes should be watching us approach," he reminded Jake and Hollyanne. And everyone. "That should get you close, and I have a badge that will get me into the building. If you are there, you can catch the door before it closes. Otherwise, we'll figure a way to disable the person on guard duty from inside."

There wasn't much more to say, so he turned and

smiled at Amanda. They started walking, like they were kinda of late getting back.

Maybe stopping to neck in the park? Something. Hopefully nobody had put two and two together.

Or he might be shot the moment he walked in that door.

CHAPTER
THIRTY

JAKE NODDED as the two lovebirds set off. He turned to Hollyanne and caught her grin. Situations like this were her specialty. She turned the other direction and set off for the next quiet alley, with him and Grant next, then Spencer and Rik trailing.

Pacific Force, on the prowl.

To the corner and look, but nobody was around. Dinner time, and the Germans took their business hours deadly serious, unlike overworked Americans.

Hollyanne went around the corner and he and Grant gave her a twenty-count head start. She could take any one person by herself, so the goal now was to not look like an assault team moving into position. Even if that was God's honest truth.

Nathaniel and Amanda were moving down the other street at a normal walk, so Hollyanne got ahead of them. Jake got to the next corner and crossed the alley, looking across to see Nathaniel just starting to cross.

Two more blocks and they were in position, a back corner on the opposite diagonal from where Nathaniel would approach.

"Anybody in sight?" he asked quietly as he caught up to Hollyanne.

"Nobody," she whispered. "Just about to make my move, as soon as they appear."

He nodded. Ten seconds later, Hollyanne took off at a hard jog, cutting in like a gray ghost.

Jake watched her vector in on the same door that Nathaniel and Amanda had turned towards. It was lit, but closed. Locked with a card reader, according to Nathaniel.

His job now was to stay back and cover her. Too many people approaching and somebody would be seen, even though all eyes were supposed to be on Nathaniel.

It took only one to sound an alarm they couldn't afford.

The duo moved casually, while Hollyanne got flat against the side of the building and slid along. Supposedly, the cameras weren't all that accurately placed, assuming a frontal approach instead of a sneak.

Cops kicking in the front door, rather than Pacific Force coming for your souls.

Nathaniel pulled out a card and waved it at the door. Amanda pulled it open. Both entered, with Hollyanne sliding right in behind them a heartbeat later.

THIRTY-ONE

HOLLYANNE PUT it down to all the martial arts training she'd done over the years. Decades. Lifetimes.

Not many people could move full speed while not making a lot of noise in the process.

Nathaniel largely ignored her, but Amanda's eyes kept glancing over, even while those two maintained a quiet chatter that was mostly just a blur of noise.

He got to the door and paused, pulling out his badge while Hollyanne slipped up next to them. The door opened with a clack and Amanda pulled it open.

She went in on their heels, taking advantage of the full foot of height to hide behind them.

"Where ya been, Moriarty?" a woman asked with a sour laugh. "Beginning to think you'd gotten cold feet. Or maybe been arrested for jaywalking."

The interior was not particularly well lit. A small reception area with a high desk to one side where a guard sat.

Hollyanne was trying to decide how to best get to the guard when Amanda pulled out her pistol and put it in the guard's face.

"Stand up or I will shoot you dead," Amanda said in a cold, hard voice. "Hands over your head. Now."

That was one way to do it.

The woman guard complied. Hollyanne moved to where she had a better view.

Average sized woman, wearing a dark blue tunic with what looked like a ghost or something as a logo over her heart. Half-mask like they did in comic books, covering the mouth and nose in black cloth.

Just like Nathaniel had expected.

Hollyanne moved around and watched the woman's flinch of surprise. Rather than take any chances, she punched the guard in the solar plexus as hard as she could, then clipped her behind the ear when the woman bent double gasping.

Out like a light.

"Keep watch," Hollyanne said, reaching for the tunic.

She could wear it and disappear around here easily enough. Nathaniel and Amanda were known. That just meant the others, but comic book villains with costuming budgets made it a little easier to penetrate their base.

"Amanda, get the door and signal the others," Nathaniel said quietly, so he must be watching the other door.

Hollyanne got the woman's tunic and mask off, then pulled out a set of zip ties and a gag to truss her. She looked under the desk, but there was no alarm button, so she just stuffed the woman underneath for now, making a note to come back for her if there was a fire or anything.

She pulled on the outfit and masked up about the time Jake came through the door.

"One down," she said, showing the others a pair of feet sticking out.

"Is there a costume shop handy we might raid?" Grant asked.

Nathaniel turned and Hollyanne was just sorry she didn't have a camera handy, because nobody would ever believe the look of stupefied confusion on his face otherwise.

Instead, he turned to Amanda.

"Shit," she muttered. "I never even thought of that. Been too focused on getting in the door without a shootout. Could it be that easy?"

Jake stepped up and nodded to her.

"You take Hollyanne and go find out," he ordered. "We'll stay here for now."

Amanda looked at him with huge eyes but got control of her face again quickly and turned to Hollyanne.

"Let's do this," she said, nodding fiercely.

The guard hadn't been armed, but Hollyanne had her stick tucked into the usual thigh pouch and the Sig tucked into her kidney under the tunic. She nodded back and followed Amanda through the inner door.

Into the villain's lair.

NATHANIEL HAD BEEN PREPARED to fail before this. To have something go wrong. To die.

Was he gun shy from the last two times he'd had to deal with Pacific Force? Getting old, like Jake had suggested?

No, just nerves. Asking Lady Nyx to commit treason with him, then watching her actually do it. And standing around with Jake and the others, all spread out now as Spencer took over the console and started typing.

"I was all set to ask for a password, but you surprised her," Spencer said after a moment. "I've got control here."

"There's an interior camera network," Nathaniel told him. "The top row of buttons toggle through them in case whoever is here needs to check something inside."

"Gotcha," Spencer replied.

Nathaniel drifted over to watch. Jake did the same from the other side. Rik watched the inner door and Grant was standing next to the exterior.

They were in pretty good shape, depending on how soon somebody needed to relieve the guard down at Spencer's feet.

"Go back one," Jake said suddenly.

Nathaniel looked closer.

"That's Lord Wraith's office," he confirmed. "I've never seen anything beyond that, so I don't think there are cameras back there. Or a back door that I am aware of. He could have built something secret, but that would be before my time."

"If we can get costumes, we can get that far," Jake said. "Are there outside cameras around back there?"

Nathaniel had to stop and consider. The perimeter had been so badly designed that he had originally intended to just rip it all out and start over.

Then he didn't care one damned bit.

"No," Nathaniel said. "I think that's a blind spot. You suppose he intentionally left a gap in case he needed to flee?"

"No idea," Jake nodded. "Rik, you slip back outside and cover that flank. Assume he can get out that corner somehow and backstop him."

"On it," the tall blonde replied, heading out the front door.

Nathaniel nodded. Professionalism at work. A team of peers and experts. No arguments. No questions.

This was the thing he'd never been able to build up himself. Those damned English hooligans of his were generally too obstinate or stupid to work like that.

One of the reasons he's wanted to recruit Lady Nyx.

But merely one of them.

"Jake, it looks like a lot of people are at dinner," Spencer spoke up now. "Rest of the space is a little empty."

Nathaniel cursed under his breath. He was too used to someone just bringing him a tray in his office because he'd been busy doing things to the electronic network.

And maybe a little too proud and arrogant to want to eat with the peons.

Too hard to forget that he didn't belong. Didn't want to be a minion in somebody's organization.

Not when he had run his own shop for so long.

Nathaniel started counting heads on the screen.

"Not counting cooks back in the kitchen, that's maybe two thirds or more of the expected occupancy. Can we take them?"

"Don't want to," Jake grinned. "Can we get around them?"

"Sure," Nathaniel replied. "Slip along the corridor to my office and we're in the other wing of the interior."

"Hollyanne, this is Jake," the man spoke aloud. "We're going the other direction right now to try to get to Lord Wraith. Large group in the dining hall right now. Some armed. Avoid if possible and meet us over there."

Nathaniel watched the man listen but didn't have an earpiece like the team did. One more thing he added to a mental list when he and Lady Nyx were off doing their own thing.

Assuming it was still a life of crime.

"Spencer, Grant, you fall in behind," Jake said now. "Nathaniel and I will lead. Pretend like you belong here if you run into anybody. Then assume violence."

Nathaniel nodded. All of them were armed, but Pacific Force wasn't known for their body count. Infrequent, but not impossible. And he had a bulletproof vest on under his shirt, same as everybody else.

Hopefully, it would help.

Honestly, he hoped that he would never need to find out because nobody was going to shoot him tonight.

Jake did, however, draw his pistol, flip off the safety, and keep it low against his thigh.

"You lead," Jake said. "You're good enough to take down anybody we run into with your bare hands, so I'm your backup if you need a gun stuck in somebody's face. That work?"

Nathaniel nodded.

Yet another thing he missed with the fools and cretins he'd been employing.

Jake McNeil—and the rest of Pacific Force—assumed that he was competent and deadly and didn't have to worry about him stepping into a punch to take someone down. Didn't have to nursemaid him.

He really needed to hire a better class of villain. Lady Nyx was just going to be the start, but nobody else who worked for Lord Wraith. That much was certain. Grim Motoko, Neon Scoundrel, and Dead Eve were all bush-league players. A-ball where you were either just hanging on, on your way down, or just passing through on your way up.

Except that Lady Nyx was the only one going to the show.

Nathaniel took a deep breath and headed inward.

Somewhere, Lord Wraith was waiting for him, preparing to destroy the world.

THIRTY-THREE

AMANDA WALKED DOWN EMPTY, dim hallways with Hollyanne Kadjar beside her, dressed in the tunic and mask the woman on guard up front had been wearing.

Pacific Force had assumed that she was in. That she would help Moriarty/Nathaniel Hoestler take out Lord Wraith and the entire organization.

Trusted her to do her part, when Wraith had treated all of the women he'd hired as groupies. Sex objects to be ogled in tight, leather pants.

Moriarty had treated her like a woman. Nathaniel Hoestler had treated her like a friend and a peer.

And had asked her to help save the world.

She had no idea what his endgame looked like, but he obviously intended to walk away when this was all done. And McNeil seemed to accept that.

Amanda didn't want to go straight. That life was completely gone. Denounced on all sides.

Hoestler had something for her, though. A new criminal gang with her as chief enforcer? That fit her style and her skills.

And she'd be playing with the big people. Pacific Force, though, would be her enemy tomorrow.

"Just down here," Amanda said, turning a corner, except that the smaller woman put a hand on her elbow.

"Message from Jake," Hollyanne whispered. "They are going the other direction now, instead of waiting. Everyone is at dinner. We should skip laundry."

Amanda nodded. They had taken two steps down the side corridor, so she retraced her steps and peeked around the corner.

Empty.

Dim.

Prior to this, the low lighting had always struck her as moody, but now she was wondering if it reflected poverty. Financial or spiritual, she wasn't sure.

Dark because they were the Dark Citizen Movement.

Seemed like hammy overacting now.

Was this response from spending just a few hours around the others to see what a top-shelf, professional organization looked like? She'd never had anything to compare Lord Wraith to before this, and he suddenly came up wanting.

"Which way?" Hollyanne whispered.

Amanda considered the internal layout of the warehouse. Organic, in the sense that whoever Lord Wraith had originally hired to do the carpentry had done one section then left. Someone else had done the next. A third and a fourth and a fifth before it was filled in, but nobody had followed the same design.

Amateurs from the Dark Citizen doing the work instead of bringing in professionals? That would fit Lord Wraith's style. Insiders, whenever possible.

Half-assing it as a result.

"This way," Amanda whispered back.

Then she squared her shoulders and stepped around the corner, Hollyanne walking in her wake.

A shadow approached from up ahead. Broad. Short. Wheezing. Brown.

Gothic Chip.

"Ah, Lady Nyx," the woman said as she waddled closer. "Where's Moriarty?"

Amanda paused as if in thought.

"I thought he was headed for food," she replied. "Did you look in the canteen?"

"Just came from there," Gothic Chip replied.

"In that case, maybe he went back to his office first?" Amanda offered, standing in such a way that Hollyanne wasn't easily visible. "Haven't seen him in a bit."

Dark hallways worked in her favor here.

"Okay, I'll look there," the woman said with an absent nod.

Amanda slipped to one side and let the wide woman pass. Hollyanne did the same.

The hallways in here were too narrow. That was part of it. Not up to fire code, because folks had been cramming in as many rooms as possible in. Everything was a little claustrophobic. Was that what had convinced Nathaniel to leave?

They started walked again.

"Jake, someone in all brown looking for Nathaniel," Hollyanne muttered. "Headed to his office now."

Amanda nodded.

Gothic Chip had never struck her as dumb. Just badly out of shape and resentful that Lord Wraith had hired pretty killers. Something Gothic Chip was not. Competent enough, but not somebody the boys ogled as she walked by.

Was that shallow thinking? Amanda worked her ass off

to have a nice ass. And a nice everything else. She'd been born pretty and tall, but a good ass was a matter of effort.

Gothic Chip probably didn't want to hear that, either.

They moved deeper into the maze.

RIK HAD CIRCLED the building quickly. Architecture wasn't her thing, but she'd memorized the map Nathaniel had drawn. Main door was along the western edge of the southern wall. This Lord Wraith punk was almost perfectly diagonal, in the northeast corner, for his personal suite.

The exterior was steel sheets, corrugated and bolted together under a dull green paint. Cheap and fast to assemble. Maybe three stories tall at the peak of the roof, but Nathaniel had said only two stories inside.

She made her way to the corner and studied things. Exterior box about eight feet tall that gave the impression of an air conditioning unit enclosure like you might have on the back of your house.

It stood out. Didn't fit, mostly because it stuck out into the alleyway and had bollards on both corners to keep trucks from clipping it as they went by.

Rik slipped right up to the edge to look, but the box seemed to be attached to the building directly.

After the fact, though, because it was smooth steel

rather than corrugated. Painted the same color but welded instead of bolted.

Installed after the fact.

Rik grinned and moved around the box, looking for a door.

There.

Chain link fence gate with vertical plastic strips woven in. Couple of smaller things that might be a swamp cooler and a portable heater, both not much bigger than the kinds of coolers she took hunting when she was going to base camp somewhere and then walk a lot.

The door had a padlock on it. Looked a little rusty, but also competent to keep her out, since she hadn't brought bolt cutters with her and Grant was inside with his lockpicks.

Rik considered looking around for a bar she could use to pry the lock, but that would move her away from this spot and honestly this looked like that back door Jake had been expecting.

Instead, she studied the chain links themselves. Galvanized steel. Basic stuff you got at a feed store. Or hardware place, she supposed.

Rik holstered the Sig and squatted down for a moment. The fencing was latched on the sides, but not the bottom. She grinned and got a good hold, standing slowly and torquing the metal as far as she could. Cheap stuff. Bent easily enough into a U-shaped gap.

She let go and got below it, crawling backwards like this was a limbo competition. Under the mesh, then up over the bar. Twisty, but not bad.

She had crap in her hair, but that wasn't anything new. Everything would need a good wash when this was done, though she doubted that either Hollyanne or Amanda would be interested in scrubbing her back.

Might have to settle for one of the guys.

Still, she was inside. AC and heat pump side by side on little risers.

Rik moved to the side of the building and found a thin seam indicating a door. No handle on this side. Hinges inside the wall. Space to open out into this little box.

Under her feet, a metal plate. Rik considered the geometry of the situation and figured that he had a secret back exit that got him in here. Hidden unless you were looking inside from the door. Pop the plate up, probably to reveal steps down to an old sewer system or something.

Tunnel for a rat to flee.

Rik settled into the gap between the two units and drew her Sig to wait.

THIRTY-FIVE

JAKE TRAILED Nathaniel through dimly lit hallways that didn't seem to be square. Or straight. Shadowed because the light fixtures were too far apart. Ceilings low. At least a lot of storage space was overhead in a second floor that had been built up. Supplies for a siege, according to Nathaniel.

"Jake, someone in all brown looking for Nathaniel," Hollyanne came over the line. "Headed to his office now."

"Nathaniel, somebody dressed in brown headed towards your office?" Jake asked quietly.

"My assistant," he nodded. "Smart, but not friendly. Assume a bad guy. We should speed up."

Jake stretched his legs as Nathaniel did the same. The place was a labyrinth, twisting and back tracking. Obviously not designed well.

Unless your goal was to make it impossible for the cops to get through to anywhere quickly and easily on their way back to your lair. In that case, it made perfect sense.

Jake just wondered why Lord Wraith hadn't built himself something higher up. Must have a secret way out the back and didn't want to be trapped if it was a raid.

At that point, the only question was if it was on the ground floor, in which case Rik could intercept him, or underground in a sewer or something, and the man might have the chance to get away.

Jake glanced back. Grant and Spencer trailing by enough to have a gap.

"Moriarty!" a female voice suddenly cut across the space. "Where have you been? Did you get it fixed?"

Jake watched a short, pale blonde in red and blue step out of a door ahead on the right. Pretty face, but he got a look and she had the crazy eyes going.

"Ah, there you are," Nathaniel said without missing a beat. "Looked for you in the kitchen and obviously you…"

Whatever the rest of the sentence might have been was irrelevant, as Nathaniel stepped into the woman with a hard right jab to the chin that sounded like a line shot up the middle in a baseball game.

The woman was out like a light and went over backwards.

"Grab her and zip her," Jake said to Grant and Spencer while he took watch.

It had sounded loud, but there was nobody immediately around. Nathaniel went through the door the woman had come from, obviously keyed up for violence, but emerged a moment later.

"Empty," he said. "Toss her in here for now. And look for more knives hidden on her body."

"Knives?" Grant asked.

"Her name is Dead Eve," Nathaniel shook his head. "Knife fetish killer. Crazy as a shithouse rat. Taking her phone into town was the excuse to get out today."

Jake nodded. At least Nathaniel was confirming whose side he was on, even if he was using violence.

Nobody in the hallway. That wouldn't last for long,

though Nathaniel had said that this hallway was mostly for officers. Him, Dead Eve, Lady Nyx, and the others. The lower-level employees were where Hollyanne had gone.

Grant and Spencer got the woman taken care of and emerged quickly.

"Six," Grant said without prompting. "Wasn't about to look closer than that."

"You and me both, buddy," Nathaniel muttered, so Jake had a pretty good idea of what kind of woman she was.

Trouble. The bad kind.

"We're close," Nathaniel said. "Stay tight at this point, because I have a feeling we'll have to rush him."

Jake nodded. He, Grant, and Spencer had pistols out. Nathaniel was looking like the criminal Moriarty, without the nice blazer he'd had earlier.

They moved.

HOLLYANNE FOLLOWED Amanda through a few more twists and turns, including a quick jaunt across an open doorway where a lot of noise indicated people at dinner. Maybe thirty, from the quick glimpse she'd gotten as she went by.

No interruption of sound, so hopefully nobody had seen the two of them and wanted to chat. Or raise an alarm.

Movement ahead, coming around a far corner, turned out to be Nathaniel, with Jake in his shadow like she was with Amanda.

They came to rest in front of a double-door that was obviously something important. *Somebody* important.

Considering the group around her, Hollyanne went for her pole, telescoping it out into a long steel rod now. Others could shoot. She would be the one to take prisoners, assuming violence.

"Will your keycard open this one?" Jake asked, indicating a sensor next to the door.

"No," Nathaniel said. "It's open during office hours,

then closed for the night when the person inside goes for dinner. Opens again for breakfast."

"Grant, you're on," Jake said.

Everyone shuffled around, but Hollyanne stayed right at the center of the door, with Amanda on her left and Jake on her right. Anyone walking around a corner right now would either barge in to demand to know what was going on or would immediately flee and raise an alarm.

Hollyanne would rely on Jake kicking the door in at that point.

Grant knelt and went to work. One panel was smooth, with posts top and bottom from the edge. The other had a handle with a key lock. Grant slipped his picks into the gap and went to work.

Hollyanne had never learned the trick of using two pieces of steel to trick a lock, but Grant had a buddy in Redmond who trained police forces on it. The team had even gone to a party a few years ago where the dude—a software developer who turned out to be a tall, goofy, relocated Englishman married to a local architect—had let everyone play with all manner of locks and tools to see how it was done.

He and Grant had nerded out excessively over good whiskey that night.

This lock didn't take Grant long to pick. He turned the handle smoothly in one hand and looked up at her. Hollyanne looked back at Jake.

"Full frontal assault, as soon as he opens it," Jake murmured.

"Grant, on three," she said, digging her toes into the cheap carpet underfoot.

He nodded.

"One. Two. Three."

Grant exploded forward, shoving the door open then

circling with it until both were out of her way. Hollyanne was in on his heels, looking at an office set up like a dentist in Kent might do it. Low counter with a gap on the right for a receptionist. Door through to the rest of the suite, as yet unknown. Leather couch and paired chairs for people waiting to talk to the boss.

And a scream like a siren wailing from overhead. Obviously, an intruder alarm. Going off. Waking up Lord Wraith. Giving him time to react.

Hollyanne took all this in and turned.

"Jake, I need that far door open now!" she ordered.

They were tactical. She had point. That meant she gave orders.

Jake holstered his pistol and got a running start, planting one foot and driving the other into the far door, right next to the handle.

Somebody hadn't bothered sinking four-inch screws into the strike plate, because the frame shattered under the assault. Jake still bounced backwards, but she'd been expecting that, slipping by him and driving inwards.

Inner suite. Another conference room of some sort, with a big table where you might plan anarchy.

Could she say that without insulting proper anarchists?

She'd have to ask one of her friends down in Oregon sometime.

Hallway straight back, with two doors on each sides and one on the end. That would be his bedroom, unless she'd caught him on the john right now.

"In!" she yelled, not pausing.

Footsteps behind her when she circled the table turned out to be Amanda, Beretta in one hand, aimed over Hollyanne's shoulder and finger alongside the trigger well rather than on the trigger itself.

Live and ready to fire.

They charged.

CHAPTER
THIRTY-SEVEN

SERGI HAD BEEN READING when the outer alarm went off. He wasn't even dressed in his Lord Wraith costume right now, having decided to relax this evening in slacks and a white cable-knit sweater.

He was upright as fast as his reflexes could move him, thankful that doors were closed between his inner rooms and the offices beyond. The sound of his office door being shattered open moved him to flight.

No time to even grab a gun, but he had cash and identity papers on him that would get him across EU borders. And he had several boxes at various banks where he could change identities as needed.

Lord Wraith might be in trouble, but Sergi Prova was a chameleon who could vanish. Assuming he could get out of the building right now.

No time to do anything but move. Fortunately, he'd been planning for this for years. Well, not planning, but preparing. Assuming the day when the Federal Police or the Americans would kick in the front door to arrest him.

Dark Citizen was big enough these days that it could

continue meandering along if he had to vanish off the face of the earth for a few days.

Sergi moved to the outer wall and unlatched the bookcase he'd personally installed between bouts of construction to the rest of the warehouse. The latch was invisible unless you knew what to look for.

Behind it, the raw steel of the building's outer skin, hidden in the shed where his personal heating and air conditioning units kept his flat comfortable, regardless of what was happening in the rest of the warehouse.

He flipped the latch lock and pressed the panel open, reaching back to pull the bookcase closed. The longer someone had to spend looking for him inside, the bigger a head start he would have to escape whatever perimeter they might have thought was sufficient to hold him.

Fools. Did you really think I hadn't planned all this long ago? Fah!

Sergi took a step forward into the dimness of the shed, standing still to let his eyes adjust to the shadows.

Movement on his right turned his head to stare in shock as a figure stood up from cover.

Big. Blonde. Female. Almost as tall as him. Wider across the shoulders.

She had a gun in one hand.

"I'm happy to just shoot you if you don't want to surrender," she offered in a classically-American accent. "Or you can turn right back around and push that door open again behind you. Bullet through the leg at this range will lame you enough for my purposes. Or I'll shoot both legs and drag you around to the front door if you make me."

From the coldness of her voice, the woman wasn't bluffing. And had been lying in wait in here. The fencing at the gate was bent badly. Crawled under it and waited like an ambush predator?

The barrel of her pistol didn't waver but did move down from his heart to perhaps his groin. Enough to make a point.

"One," she counted slowly. "Two…"

"Okay," Sergi said, raising his hands.

The crazy bitch looked like she might enjoy shooting him. And hadn't called herself a cop or identified herself as belonging to any agency.

Who the fuck was she?

"Then turn around, sweetums," she ordered in a voice like a rusty broadsword. "Open the door. Or bleed and I'll kick it in for you."

Sergi gulped at the raw violence in her eyes. The joy at it. Almost as bad a Dead Eve or Grim Motoko, and they were both crazy women.

He turned slowly, reaching a hand in.

"Delicately, princess," the woman warned him, not moving any closer but tracking him like a missile battery.

Sergi nodded and reached with a hand, unlatching the bookcase again and pushing it into the room.

Another woman stood there. Tiny, but a whirlwind as she grabbed his wrist and used some twisting Judo throw that had him in the room, on his back, and staring up at her before he knew what happened.

Sergi looked back and up and saw the blonde step to the door with a smile.

"We got trouble coming?" she asked.

Yelled, really, over the ongoing siren.

Sergi smiled. They might have captured him, but apparently his entire goon squad was still out there.

He'd be free again shortly in that case.

AMANDA WATCHED Hollyanne Kadjar flip Lord Wraith and stand over him. One down. But that left the other killers. They would react to that door alarm by running for the armory.

She had an idea, though. Jake McNeil was right next to her. As was Grant Collingwood.

"Is the outer door still locked, if someone pulls it shut?" she yelled over the sirens.

"Yes," he yelled back.

"I need to go distract all the men and women outside," she told Jake. "Get them running for their lives instead of coming to rescue this shit."

"How?" he asked, starting to walk with her because Amanda was already in motion. Nathaniel was with her, while the other four stayed with the prisoner.

Lord Wraith's time was done. She needed to make sure Pacific Force could get out of here later.

"They know me," she said as they got closer to the alarm. "I can bluff them."

"Are you sure?" Nathaniel asked.

That warmed her. He didn't see this as a forlorn hope.

Amanda wasn't sure she agreed, but she had to try.

"I am," she replied.

"Run if you have to, to lead them away, then," he nodded. "I have your number."

Amanda nodded. He was making sure she got away right now, even if Jake and the others took Nathaniel into custody.

She found herself looking forward to his call.

"Stand clear of the door," she ordered the others, moving them out of sight.

Then she grabbed the handle, Beretta in one hand and emerged.

Already, goons were approaching from her right. She pulled it shut and confronted them.

"Son of a bitch planted a bomb and fled," she yelled at the top of her lungs, even though it was quieter on this side. "Told me to fuck off and die when the police got here. We have three minutes and thirty seconds before the whole building catches fire. You, is the fire alarm still disconnected?"

One of the goons in blue tunics and a mask looked up at her like a frog staring into a flashlight at night.

"Ya-yes," he stammered.

"Fuck!" Amanda yelled. "And fuck him. Every one of you for himself then. Unless you want to die when all this is on fire!"

Rather than wait on any sort of democratic consensus, Amanda bulled her way through the assembled mass, using her height and gun to clear a path, then running.

Those behind her were still uncertain.

"It's gonna blow!" she yelled at the newest group to arrive, these new ones armed with machine pistols. "Fire! Get out while you can!"

They stared at her blankly, but Amanda felt the first

stirrings of panic catch, infecting one, then the next. One of the women turned and started to jog away from her, yelling *Fire!* at everyone.

As badly designed and tight as all these corridors were, being trapped in a fire was a serious fear she'd had. Obviously, so had the others, because pretty quickly others were clomping loudly in her wake.

Panic was an infectious disease. Especially in a closed space.

The group behind her turned into a mob. The mob wanted out. Amanda ran for all she was worth, yelling *Fire!* as she went. Others took up the call, infecting others like hot embers on a hard wind.

She was in better shape than most, because she worked at it and jogged a lot. Even then, it was hard staying ahead of the wave that wanted to overwhelm her and drive her to the bottom of the sea. More than once, somebody almost caught her from behind, drowning men and women wanting to pull her down to get by her.

Amanda got to the outer door and burst through it. For one idle moment, she considered sliding to the side so that she might rest, but feared that others might do the same. At some point, they would come to their senses and realize that they'd been had. Especially when the building stubbornly refused to burn down.

Hopefully, Jake was calling the police right now. Or better, somebody running behind her had gotten to some level of autopilot and dialed emergency services to call in a fire alarm.

She ran for all she was worth.

Nathaniel would call her.

CHAPTER
THIRTY-NINE

JAKE TURNED TO GRANT, but the man was already standing on a coffee table he'd pulled over, fussing with the overhead speaker. A moment later, he ripped it out of the ceiling and jerked the wires out of the back. The noise fell to nothing.

Jake felt better immediately. He glanced back, but Rik and Hollyanne had Lord Wraith in custody. Zipped and gagged. Trussed like Sunday dinner, as it were.

He nodded and turned to Nathaniel. That man was standing at the door listening intently. A moment later, he pulled out his pistol, holding it out of sight as he pulled the door open and peeked out.

"Clear here," he said, closing it again. "Whatever she did worked. At least for now. Now what?"

Jake turned to look back down the hallway.

"You ladies need anything?" he called down the long hallway.

"Negative," Hollyanne replied.

"Keep him tight," Jake yelled, then turned to Spencer and dropped his voice to a whisper. "You and Nathaniel able to hack this system from here?"

There was a monitor on the desk and a sleek tower underneath. Both men nodded and got to work.

"How long until somebody gets smart?" Spencer asked.

"If you lock the outer door and change all the codes, nobody can get back in," Jake answered. "But we need to get that one woman from under the desk. Grant, you watch the door. I'll be back."

He walked to the space where Lord Wraith had been pulled into a chair and zip-tied to it. Wallet, cash, and knives were nearby on a table next to Rik, so she'd frisked the man.

Jake focused on Hollyanne.

"Need you to run a quick sweep in costume and see if you can get any stragglers out of the building," he said. "That includes the one under the front desk."

"Got it," she said, immediately moving past him.

He heard her talk to Spencer and Nathaniel up front, so probably back to watching interior cameras.

Whatever Amanda had done, hopefully it had been sufficient. Although Lord Wraith did have a back door he had almost fled through, but for Rik.

Jake studied the man now. Tall. Rangy. Shaved skull. Blond beard Nathaniel had said was probably a dye job. Sharp eyes.

Jake would have guessed the man to be about sixty now. Old enough to know better, but some folks never grow up.

He reached out and pulled down the cloth that someone had tied around his mouth to keep him quiet.

Lord Wraith looked like he'd sucked on a lemon. Jake smiled.

"You can save me a lot of hassle by talking," Jake offered evenly. "If I have to take your entire computer system apart first, I'm likely to be really cranky by the time I call the Federal Police to come for you."

"Who are you?" Lord Wraith snarled. "And who the hell do you think you are, doing this to me?"

"I'm Jake McNeil," he replied coldly. "That's Rik Farrell. Hollyanne Kadjar was the one in costume. Grant Collingwood and Spencer Sargossian are out front breaking into your computer system right now."

Jake could tell the man recognized the names by the way his eyes got huge and his mouth fell open.

"Pacific Force," he whispered. "How?"

"One of the women you hired was a double agent," Jake lied with a breezy smile. "Waited until the right moment and called us in. Apparently, she didn't agree with your plans."

Helped, lying that one of his women had done it. Nathaniel had mentioned that all four of Lord Wraith's top killers presented as female, as did more than half his staff in the building.

Redirected his ire away from the truth.

"You can't stop me!" Lord Wraith snapped.

"Oh, I can," Jake shook his head. "You can make it easy so I only have to make one phone call. Or you can be a pain in my ass and I have to tell everyone. That's going to cost most of them a lot of money, so I imagine more than one might want to extradite you later. I won't care at that point because I'll have turned you over to someone. Maybe the highest bidder tomorrow. We'll see. Feel like telling me something that won't make me dangle you out there for the Russians and the Indians?"

Rather than wait for an answer, Jake turned and walked away from the man. Let him stew for now.

He headed up front.

"How are we doing?" he asked Spencer.

"Building appears empty at this point," Spencer replied.

"How about the other business?"

"It will take a while to get through all those systems to find the data we need," Nathaniel said. "He had a private server back here that I wasn't aware of. Something Gothic Chip must have set up on a separate router from the main one I controlled."

"Where is it physically?" Jake asked.

"Probably back in his room," Nathaniel said. "In a server closet most likely."

"We need to disconnect it from everything," Jake said. "Now. If she set it up, she might be able to get into it remotely and wipe it."

"Shit," Nathaniel growled. "Spencer, you go with him so I'm not seen. Thank you for that, Jake. I was listening."

"Anytime," Jake nodded.

He grabbed Spencer and they jogged back to the back, looking in each of the four rooms. One of them was configured as an office, with a small tower for blade servers, about the size of a dorm refrigerator.

Jake stepped back as Spencer crawled around behind it and started tracing wires.

"We want it remote or off?" Spencer asked.

Jake considered his options. He wasn't nearly the computer nerd he's been in high school, but still wrote code occasionally. Mostly to learn new languages and keep up with tech.

"Let's just pull the power and assume that the person who built it did a good enough job," he decided.

"Going down," Spencer laughed.

The whole assembly had been humming with fans but stopped suddenly as Spencer pulled plug after plug out of the back, including the router on top.

"Six blades," Spencer noted, standing again. "Hell of a lot of horsepower for a rinky-dink operation like this."

"That's why disconnecting it probably wasn't enough," Jake nodded. "There's a whole lot more here than meets the eye. And I don't want to risk somebody triggering a job to overwrite it seven times when nobody is looking. This way, it's preserved. You have the passwords?"

"Added myself and a default with superadmin privileges, then downgraded everybody else to regular users," Spencer grinned. "They have about as many rights as a VAX terminal user at that point, but I agree that somebody might have buried a landmine somewhere. Only takes once. So now what?"

"You head back up with Grant and keep watch," Jake said. "Hollyanne can stay up there with you when she gets back, but she can also patrol in case we missed somebody."

"Got it."

Jake watched him go, then headed back to talk to Lord Wraith again.

"I turned your server off," Jake smiled down at the man. "And killed the router it was connected to. Shortly, I'll have to call some friends in German Intelligence and turn you and it over to them. Feel like talking, or feel like sitting in a small concrete box for a while? No? Nothing? Suit yourself, then."

Jake reached into his pocket and pulled out his cell phone, dialing a number.

"This is Steve," the British agent answered quickly.

"Jake McNeil," he replied. "You still on vacation?"

"I am," Steve replied.

His name wasn't Steve, but he also didn't exist. Worked reasonably well in this industry.

"I'm about to call Johann and Dieter," Jake said,

giving Steve an address. "If you happened to be here at the time, they might not immediately throw you out of the building. Especially if you called your boss and told him we had someone he might want to extradite at some point."

"I'll be there in fifteen minutes," Steve replied.

"See you then," Jake smiled and hung up. "Spencer and Grant, Steve will be here in a few minutes."

Then he scrolled through the contacts on his phone until he found the one he wanted.

"Jake?" Johann asked as he answered. "What's up?"

Jake gave him an address.

"I have somebody in custody," Jake said. "And all his computer systems, but you'll want to relocate them to a safe lab before you power them back up. I'd bring along a team of agents, a few supervisors, and maybe an Assistant Director when you come. Doubt you'll need guns, but only because we scattered all the mice before we captured the rat. Still, you should hurry because I had previously promised British Intelligence that they could be here, and somebody is in route now."

"Got it, Jake," Johann replied. "I'm in Berlin right now, but Dieter is local. I'll call him immediately. Can you give me more?"

"Not over the phone," Jake said. "But we're in the process of stopping another madman who wants to destroy the world. And you'll have primary jurisdiction when you get all the stories."

Jake hung up and smiled down at Lord Wraith.

"The only thing you can give me right now that I care about is the identity of the rocket itself," Jake scowled. "Everything else is going to be governmental, so hopefully you don't have assassins coming after you when this is all said and done."

Lord Wraith scowled back.

"Why do you work for those capitalist pigs?" he demanded.

"Who's paying you to do this?" Jake fired right back. "You didn't come up with the idea yourself. You're just the vector of chaos some other filthy capitalist pig is paying in his own private war. Your hands are dirtier than mine because I'm not lying about my motivations. I'm not sleeping with the enemy and letting him use me. I'm an agent. You're just a tool."

Jake turned and walked away again. Mostly so he didn't slap the dumb son of a bitch across the face right now. He got to the door when Lord Wraith muttered a word.

Jake paused and looked back expectantly.

"Next Tuesday," Lord Wraith repeated it louder.

Jake nodded.

Assuming the man wasn't lying, they knew which launch it was supposed to be. And where to look in the records for the evidence.

"Let's hope you're telling me the truth," Jake said, walking away.

Steve and Dieter would both be here soon enough.

NATHANIEL WATCHED Jake emerge from the back. He'd been listening with half an ear to the conversation back there. Sounded like Jake had what he needed. Just to be certain, Nathaniel had written down all his own usernames and passwords for the outer system to go with the ones Spencer had added into the captured one.

Jake appeared now, nodding for Nathaniel to join him by the door. Grant drifted off, then walked out to stand in back with Rik guarding the prisoner.

"Spencer, is the place empty?" Jake asked.

"As far as I can tell," Spencer replied. "Hollyanne is still sweeping, but nobody stayed outside the front door when Amanda led them out. Rats and sinking ships. Hollyanne got the last one and that woman took off like someone was chasing her with a scourge."

"Good enough," Jake nodded, then turned back to Nathaniel and spoke quietly. "Next Tuesday."

"Heard that," Nathaniel replied. "Do we trust it?"

"No, but at this point he's in custody, so I expect he's trying to buy some slack. Pacific Force has a rep that's better than most. If he'd messed with the Russians or

Indians, they might have killed him in prison, failure or not. Right now, it's a group of billionaires arguing penis size with each other. The US government will want to be involved, mostly because they have jurisdiction over those launches. The Brits just don't want to be left out. The Germans will hold him while people bid."

"Now what?" Nathaniel asked hesitantly.

They'd danced around this topic all day.

Was all this good enough for Jake to let him go?

There were an amazing number of nations with warrants for his arrest. And a few with bounties significant enough to draw the eye.

"Now?" Jake asked.

Nathaniel nodded.

"Now, I think your girlfriend has one hell of a head start on you," Jake grinned. "Don't want her getting too far away, do you?"

"I do not," Nathaniel sighed.

"Got funds handy?" Jake asked.

"I have a box in my office with a false bottom," Nathaniel nodded. "If I can grab that, I'm set."

Jake nodded and smiled. Then turned to Spencer.

"Keys?" he asked.

Nathaniel watched Spencer pull out a ring and toss it over. Nathaniel caught it automatically, brain not quite processing.

"It's a rental," Jake said. "Paperwork is in the glove compartment if you wanted to return it to the airport early."

"Just like that?" Nathaniel asked, still waiting for the other shoe to drop.

"Just like that," Jake nodded. "Sometime next week we'll be after you again, but that gives you time to get to ground first. Maybe make a phone call and have that coffee date you were muttering about. She's English, though I'm guessing we only need to pass through London barely long enough to brief Sir William and then head back to Seattle and take a long weekend so we don't cramp you."

Nathaniel absorbed the words, but it took him a moment to fully grasp. Nobody was going to stop him walking out that door. Getting into the sedan and driving to the airport.

Simply disappearing.

Then he squared his shoulders and nodded. Held out his hand for Jake to take in a firm grip.

"Some days, I'm sorry that it ended up like this," he told Jake, once his closest friend in the world. "But I'm glad that you took my call. Can't say that I'm looking forward to needing to do that again, but it's good to know."

"Likewise," Jake said. "If you ever do decide to retire, maybe we can get a beer sometime. Or if you find yourself in Seattle and have an afternoon off."

"Thank you," Nathaniel said.

He slipped through the double door into the dimness beyond and started planning his escape.

FORTY-ONE

JAKE WATCHED HIM GO.

"Hollyanne, Nathaniel will be passing by you at some point, if you want to give him a hug before he goes," Jake said aloud.

"Understood," she replied in his ear.

Jake nodded. Checked his watch.

Ten minutes until all hell broke loose out there, but Jake wasn't worried about Nathaniel getting away. Dieter wouldn't bring enough people to box everything in initially. All the mice had needed time to scatter so as to distract from Amanda and Nathaniel getting away in the chaos.

That much he'd promised the man, because this one had been big enough, scary enough, to step past all the grief they'd caused each other over the years.

The law might take a dim view of such things, but Lord Wraith hadn't seen Nathaniel at the end. And likely believed Jake when he said that one of his women killers had betrayed him. He had a one in four chance of being almost right, too.

But hopefully, Pacific Force had saved the day.

Jake walked over to where Spencer had been furiously typing on the keyboard.

"What have you got?" Jake asked.

"HR files," Spencer grinned. "You want personnel files, payroll, or banking?"

"Copy it all," Jake said. "We'll have to make copies available to a half dozen agencies in the next twelve hours. Might as well get some brownie points for doing it ourselves. Any luck tracking down leads on next Tuesday?"

"That was how I found the banking directory," Spencer nodded. "The numbers look hinky to me. Like maybe somebody was spoofing things when making transfers in, but nobody here understood the systems well enough to raise alarms."

"Any clue who might be behind it?" Jake asked.

"Most of these transfers originate in Moscow banks, Jake," Spencer said, turning serious now. "If an American billionaire was really involved, that would be about the last place he'd do it, unless he'd routed it from a Cayman's bank through Switzerland and Jersey. We'd be talking half a dozen proxies at a minimum. Maybe somebody wanted to hide his tracks that well, but maybe not. Consider the political situation."

Indeed. Nobody could be sure if the Russians owned the American President in fee simple these days, but it certainly looked that way. Why they'd want to destroy the world was a whole other conversation, unless they saw the writing on the wall from private industry being able to launch rockets into orbit.

Nobody would need the Russians for anything at that point.

Were they willing to burn the whole world down rather than lose gracefully?

Jake didn't know.

But he did know that Pacific Force would continue to be there when they were needed.

Too many crazy people out there these days.

READ MORE

To read more of my fiction, sign up for my newsletter. You'll also get a free book!

http://www.blazeward.com/newsletter/

ABOUT THE AUTHOR

Blaze Ward is a prolific Indie writer and publisher who works mostly in Science Fiction and Light Thriller, with occasional forays into lots of other genres like superheroic fantasy.

You can find more of his titles at www.blazeward.com/books, www.KnottedRoadPress.com and wherever else you buy your books.

He also edits Boundary Shock Quarterly, an SF magazine he founded in 2018, and Thrill Ride Magazine.

ABOUT KNOTTED ROAD PRESS

Knotted Road Press publishes dynamic fiction set in exotic locations. Our authors cover a wide range of genres including science fiction, fantasy, mystery, literary, and poetry. We also have unique non-fiction voices in genres such as autobiography, business, cookbooks, and how-tos. We offer both DRM-free ebooks and print books for a global readership.

www.KnottedRoadPress.com

www.ingramcontent.com/pod-product-compliance
Lightning Source LLC
Chambersburg PA
CBHW071526120726
47907CB00013B/1081